Bouncey the Elf and Friends

Brian Leo Lee

ISBN-13: 978-1516870998

By Brian Leo Lee
(Children's stories)
Just Bouncey
Bouncey the Elf and Friends Meet Again
Bouncey the Elf and Friends Together Again

Mr Tripsy's Trip
Mr Tripsy's Boat Trip

By Brian Leon Lee
Trimefirst
Domain of the Netherworld

All available as Paperback or eBooks

About the Author

The author was born in Manchester. On leaving school, a period in accountancy was followed by a teaching career in Primary Education.

Several years of telling his own stories to his two, then young children, when on camping holidays, led to the development of his many story characters.

Now retired, living in South Yorkshire.

http://www.bounceytheelf.co.uk

For

Rita, Karen and Stephen

Contents

Bouncey the Elf
and the Treasure of Mirror Lake

Bouncey the Elf woke with a sleepy groan. He wondered what had disturbed him.

A glow from his bedroom window caught his eye. Looking outside Bouncey saw a strange sight. Sitting on his magic flying carpet was his friend, the Wizard.

'Bouncey! Bouncey!' cried the Wizard. 'Come down right away.'

As quickly as he could Bouncey, went downstairs to his front door.

'What do you want?' he asked. 'It's three o'clock in the morning.'

'Sorry! Bouncey,' replied the Wizard, 'but you must go to Mirror Lake, right now!'

'What for?' said Bouncey, in a puzzled voice.

'The Goblins have found out about the secret treasure of the lake,' the Wizard said excitedly.

'We can't let the Goblins take it, you must stop them, Bouncey.'

'Me. Me. Why me?' screeched Bouncey in alarm.

'You are the only elf who knows the way through to the Barren Mountains and then to Mirror Lake.'

'Well, if it is so important, I suppose I shall have to,' said Bouncey, not happy at the thought of getting up in the middle of the night.

'Well, I can't stay. I have to search for a few frogs' legs, bats wings and some snake's eyes for a little spell I am making.

'Bye, bye,' called the Wizard as he zoomed away on his amazing magic flying carpet.

Bouncey did not waste a minute.

He grabbed his backpack, quickly filling it with what he might need for his trip: A lightweight sleeping bag, spare clothes, a bottle of water, several energy bars and packets of biscuits, pen– knife, a waterproof box of matches, a thin but strong, coil of rope and a map of Elfinland.

It was still dark, as Bouncey went through the village, quietly creeping past the Elf King's Palace, making sure not to disturb any of the palace guards.

Bouncey soon reached the bridge over the River of Dreams without any trouble.

He crossed the bridge and went deep into Fawn Wood. It was dark and a little scary, especially when, an owl suddenly hooted.

Too Wit! Too Woo! Too Wit! Too Woo!

Then Bouncey found that he could see more clearly. The sun had risen and he felt much better.

Following a path through the trees of Fawn Wood, Bouncey took care not to disturb a herd of deer quietly grazing in a sunny glade.

To save time, Bouncey decided to take a short cut. It could be dangerous. He was going to pass through a part of the Wild Boar Forest.

First of all, though, he had to cross the River of Dreams again. Finding a part of the river, in which had been set a path of stepping - stones, Bouncey started to cross.

'Oh no!' cried Bouncey as he slipped off a stone and splashed into the river.

The river was quite deep and Bouncey was swept downstream, struggling to keep his head above the water.

Just when he thought that he could not stop himself from

sinking, his backpack snagged a branch, which was hanging down over the river.

Wow, thought Bouncey, *that was a close escape.*

By pulling himself along the hanging branch, Bouncey managed to reach the bank of the river.

'Oooahh,' said Bouncey, shivering. 'I'd better dry off and change into some dry clothes.'

He picked up a few sticks lying under a tree and quickly fetched out his box of matches.

Soon, Bouncey had a roaring fire going and had changed into his spare dry clothes. His wet things were put over a nearby bush to dry from the heat of the fire.

Now nicely settled, Bouncey had something to eat and drink.

'Ahhh! That's better!' said Bouncey, lying back against a tree trunk, warming his hands by the fire.

A rustling noise suddenly broke the silence. Bouncey looked around in alarm.

Through the bushes and trees, the outline of a large animal could just be seen.

A snort, a sound of snuffling then a loud squeal, made Bouncey jump.

'Oh no!' Bouncey groaned to himself.' 'It's not a wild boar. Is it?'

It was.

Now, Bouncey had had many narrow escapes before and his quick wits had often saved him.

So, quick as a flash, Bouncey picked up a blazing branch and threw it towards the wild boar.

Wild boars, like most wild animals are afraid of fire and so this one did what any sensible animal would do.

It ran away.

The blazing branch fortunately, soon went out.

'Flips' said Bouncey.

'I think I had better get as far away from here as soon as possible.'

So without any more delay, Bouncey put out the fire by throwing loose earth over the flames. He then packed his backpack with all his now, dry things.

Bouncey decided to walk along the side of the river, hoping to find a small boat, which would make travelling much easier and faster.

Some time later, he found just what he wanted. By the side of the river were several canoes.

The only problem was that, as Bouncey well knew, they belonged to the Goblins.

'I must be near the Goblins Lair.' said Bouncey to himself. 'I shall have to be very quiet.'

After checking that there were no Goblins about, Bouncey 'borrowed' one of the canoes.

Being so small, his backpack fitted into the canoe quite easily.

How much easier it was paddling down the river in the 'borrowed' Goblins canoe but Bouncey still had to take great care.

Lower down the River of Dreams was the heartland of the Goblins, the Elves' enemy.

The Goblins mined gold and diamonds near here and they often took lost elves as slaves to work in their mines.

Sure enough, as Bouncey paddled quietly past the mountains filled with gold and diamonds, he could hear the faint, clink! clink! The noise of picks and other tools being used in the Goblin mines.

That night Bouncey made camp by the river. After making a fire and having some food and drink, he settled into his sleeping bag, with a big sigh of relief.

'I'm so tired with all that paddling. I could sleep for a week.'

The next morning, he wasted not a second. Within twenty minutes he was away, paddling along the river towards the Barren Mountains.

Many years ago, some elves say hundreds of years ago; there was a war between the Wardens of Wizards and the Witches Covens.

They both used very powerful spells to try to win the war - lightning, fireballs, storms, floods and drought.

The Wizards had won, but in the place known as the Barren Mountains nothing grows.

Nothing at all!

Then, away to his right, far into the hills, Bouncey thought he saw a flash of light.

I wonder if that is the Wizard in his cave, making more of his special magic spells.

Now entering the Barren Mountains, Bouncey knew he had to take special care. He might meet the Goblins.

Soon afterwards, he had to leave his 'borrowed' Goblin canoe on the bank by the river and making sure he had filled his water bottle; he put on his backpack and set off.

It was a long hot dry walk. No trees to give shade, no grass or flowers to make the way look pleasant. Just bare grey rock and lots of tiny loose stones, which kept getting into his shoes.

'Oh flips' said Bouncey, getting a bit annoyed.

'Why did I agree to come on this trip? It's horrible.'

Then, just as he had feared, he heard the horrible sounds of –

Wah! Wah! Wah!

The Goblins had arrived.

I've got to escape and quickly, he thought, *but how?*

Now Bouncey knew the Barren Mountains better than any other elf in Elfinland. What if he could make the Goblins follow his tracks, deep into the Barren Mountains where there was no water and then find a place to hide.

'It's worth a try' said Bouncey to himself. So, keeping as low as he could, Bouncey made a trail of his footprints in the dust, so clear, that anyone could see them.

He went deeper and deeper into the Barren Mountains, up and down so many different valleys, that even he thought he might get lost.

Eventually he found a good place to hide, a hollow between two big rocks. Now his idea was put to the test.

He dropped his backpack onto the ground and pulled out his sleeping bag. It was the same colour as the rocks all around him. Once inside the sleeping bag no one could see him. Not even the Goblins.

They passed by soon afterwards, many of them shouting out that they were thirsty.

Later that day, Bouncey, so thankful that he had remembered to fill his water-bottle earlier that morning, set off for Mirror Lake. Thankfully he didn't see one Goblin.

It was evening time when he finally reached Mirror Lake. Tired from all his walking, he sat down for a rest, before going for a closer look.

What a sight it was.

The water was so still. It really looked like a mirror. The lake surface reflected everything so clearly, that Bouncey nearly fell into it.

'Now that I am here, what do I do to find the treasure?'

He thought and he thought. Then, he had an idea.

Many years ago he remembered, an old witch had told him that anyone skimming a pebble across the Mirror Lake, making eleven skips at one go, would make something strange happen.

Would it work though?

All I have to do is throw them to make them skip eleven times.

Carefully taking aim, Bouncey threw the first pebble. Splash!

No skip at all. 'Oh flips!'

This is much harder than I thought.

He tried again. 'Hooray!' Five skips.

He threw two more times, the best throw being eight skips.

'Oh no, I've only got one pebble left.'

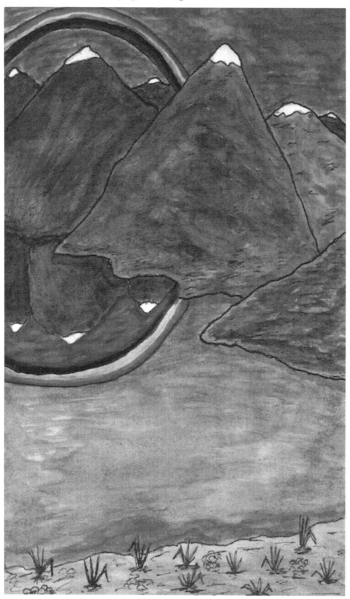

This time, before throwing, Bouncey crouched down to one side, moving his arm right back.

Then throwing as fast as he could, he flicked his wrist as he let go of the pebble.

The pebble hit the lake surface and began skipping along the water. One, two... Five... eight... ten... eleven.

'It made eleven!' cried Bouncey excitedly.

He watched as the lake surface suddenly began to bubble and steam spouted upwards in a thick cloud.

Bouncey couldn't see a thing. He was surrounded by it. Then the steam cleared and he saw a large silvery seashell floating on the surface of the lake.

It was so big Bouncey could easily have ridden inside it.

Lying on the inside of the silvery shell was an open, golden casket.

Bouncey gasped and said, 'Oh my, it can't be,' when he saw what was inside the golden casket.

A magical Unicorn Horn.

Anyone who owned the magical Unicorn Horn would be protected from all evil things, with this, Elfinland would be safe, forever, from the Goblins.

'How can I carry this treasure safely back to my village?'

He suddenly had a brilliant idea.

After he had managed to get the golden casket and Unicorn Horn safely to the edge of the lake. Bouncey piled every thing that could be burned, including his backpack, into a heap and set fire to the lot.

Shortly afterwards, he spied the Wizard, flying towards him on his magic carpet.

'Hi, Bouncey,' called the Wizard.

'When I saw some smoke coming from the Barren Mountains, I thought you might be in trouble with the Goblins. So I came as fast as I could.'

17

'My word, what's that? - Is it the treasure of Mirror Lake?' cried the Wizard with excitement as he saw the magical Unicorn Horn.

'Yes it is.' replied Bouncey, grinning with pleasure that he had found it. He then asked the Wizard for a favour.

'Please, can you give me a lift back to my village?'

'Of course I can,' said the still excited Wizard helping Bouncey on-board. The magic carpet carried them back to the Elf Village in no time at all.

How surprised the Elf King was when he saw the Unicorn Horn.

Bouncey became a celebrity for days. Best of all, he liked the Elf King's offer to be able take whatever he fancied from the Royal Kitchens for a whole week.

He really liked the jellybean surprise, the strawberry cupcakes, the slices of cake with jello-filling and chocolate, the peanut butter - banana smoothie, and the ice - cream sundae and that was only the first day.

Do you think Bouncey the Elf was a little bit too greedy?

Henry the Caravan
and the Troublesome Family

Henry the Caravan was waiting for the new seasons visitors. After having been repaired during the winter and receiving a new coat of paint, he was really sparkling at the start of the summer season.

'I wonder what sort of family I'll get for this first visit.' he asked himself. He waited and waited. Cars came by... but didn't stop.

Oh dear! I hope I haven't been forgotten, he thought sadly.

Suddenly, a car screeched to a halt by his front gate. A Mum, Dad and three children got out of the car. The children began jumping about shouting, at each other.

'Come on kids,' shouted Dad. 'Help with the luggage.'

'Oh! - You do it Dad,' said the eldest - a boy who was about ten years old. He ran up to the gate, kicked it open, nearly knocking it off its hinges.

The two little girls ran after him, screaming. 'Oh! Look at those lovely flowers, Mum.'

They then began to pull up several flowers growing alongside the path - of course they weren't there to be picked up.

Henry didn't know what to think. He was so shocked by their behaviour.

The boy went up to the caravan door and yanked the handle, much too hard. The door did not move. He then kicked the door, hard.

'Ouch!' exclaimed Henry to himself, 'That hurt!'

'Hey! Dad! The door's locked,' shouted the boy.

'Try the handle again, you silly boy,' snapped Dad.

The boy turned the handle more carefully this time and the door opened.

'Kids!' moaned Dad.

He struggled with three large suitcases. Then, staggering up the steps and through the door, he dropped the suitcases onto the caravan floor.

Cripes! Thought Henry. These people don't seem to bother about anybody's feelings.

Then Mum came in with some more luggage and the two girls followed her into the caravan.

'Now.' Mum said. 'Where can we put those flowers? 'Let me see…'

She began to open the cupboards and in one of them found a lovely vase.

'Ooh! Look at this!' she exclaimed. Then it slipped through her clumsy fingers and smashed into lots of little pieces on the floor.

'Bother!' Mum said, as she kicked the bits under the table.

'Oh No! My best vase and she's not even bothering to pick up the pieces,' muttered Henry to himself.

Meanwhile the sisters had discovered the seats and had begun to jump up and down on them --- up and down --- up and down.

'If they don't stop they're going to give me a headache!' groaned Henry.

'Dad! Dad! Look at this, Dad. It's like being on a tambourine!' shouted the youngest girl excitedly.

'A trampoline - you silly girl,' replied Dad. 'And stop jumping on there - it's a seat.'

'Oh Dad!' grumbled the girls but they sat down quietly on the seat.

'Well now, we'd better get something to eat,' said Mum. She got out some biscuits and then started to make bread and peanut - butter sandwiches.

The children grabbed the biscuits first. 'I don't like these, Mum, complained one of the sisters and she threw them onto the floor.

Aaaagh, thought Henry. *What messy kids and no manners at all.*

Dad was thirsty and wanted a drink, so he asked the boy to fill the kettle.

He gave a big groan. 'Why me, Dad?'

'Because I asked you too, now hurry up!' shouted Dad.

Going to the sink, the boy turned the tap full on and water splashed out of the kettle, spraying everywhere, especially onto the carpet, which had just been cleaned for the summer season.

'Oh! Look at my carpet.' cried Henry to himself. No one bothered to mop it up.

Then Mum made some tea. Dad said he wanted lots of sugar in his cup.

So Mum picked up the bag of sugar but it slipped out of her hands and burst on the floor. Sugar spread all over, mixing with the water on the carpet.

Henry could hardly look.

'I suppose I will have to clean that up,' groaned Mum. She got a cloth and dabbed the carpet and seemed to make an even bigger mess than before.

Henry gasped. 'Oh! What a ….! What a family! I must do something to stop them staying here.'

Meanwhile the sisters were jumping around again on the seats. 'We want to go to bed,' they chanted. They wanted to try out their new sleeping bags.

So Dad started to change the seats into beds. He had no sooner got the cushions arranged when the girls immediately started jumping up and down on them.

Then the two sisters began to have a pillow fight. Before you knew it, they had knocked an ornament off a table and then a lovely framed photograph of the campsite, fell off the wall.

What on earth are they going to do next! I can't imagine, thought Henry.

Soon the whole family started to get tired and after a lot of shouting, fussing and squabbling, the beds were made up and they all fell asleep.

Henry decided to stay awake, to try to think of a plan to get rid of this troublesome family. By the next morning he was ready to act.

The family awoke next morning, sleepy and grumpy. Dad wanted a cup of tea in bed. So Mum went to the sink to fill the kettle but there was no water coming from the tap.

Henry wouldn't let any water pass through it.

'Water's off,' said Mum.

'Oh bother!' grumbled Dad.

'Now then, lad, you will have to go and get some water from the tap outside. Will you get the water carrier, please.'

The boy pulled faces and moaned that he didn't want to and why couldn't his sisters do it.

Dad shouted at him in a great, booming voice, which sent him scuttling to the door.

The boy tried to open the door, but the door wouldn't open.

Henry was making sure the door would not open.

The boy pulled and pulled - then Dad tried as well, but it simply wouldn't open.

'All right' said Dad.

'Let's forget about the tea for now - we'll have something to eat.'

So Mum went to the cupboard where she'd put some food the night before but the cupboard door was shut fast.

Henry wouldn't let the cupboard door open either.

24

The girls started chanting. 'We're hungry! We're hungry!'

'Be quiet,' shouted Dad at the top of his voice. The children quietened down - they could tell he was quite annoyed.

'Well,' Dad said in a strained voice, trying to keep calm. 'We'd better open the window and shout for help.'

He tried to open the window - it wouldn't budge.

Henry wouldn't let it, of course.

Dad was starting to get a little worried - everything was stuck and there was no food or water to be had.

Even the games cupboard, to keep the children busy, wouldn't open.

'There's something weird about this caravan,' said Dad.

The family all hurriedly got dressed and sorted the beds back into seats again. Then they sat down to think of what to do next.

Henry then made the seat cushions slide onto the floor and the whole family fell down in a heap, all arguing about who had done it.

Just then the family saw the campsite Warden going by.

They caught his attention by banging on the window.

The campsite Warden came up to the window. 'Yes,' he mouthed.

Dad kept banging on the window and looking frantic.

The campsite Warden thought he had better investigate. He went around to the front door of Henry the Caravan and walked inside.

Dad looked at the campsite Warden in amazement.

'We've been stuck in here for ages,' he spluttered. 'We've got no water coming from the taps, the door wouldn't open and neither would the windows or cupboards.'

'Look!' complained Dad.

He pulled at the games cupboard door with all his might - it opened easily, because Henry let it.

Dad ended up on the floor covered in games of snakes and ladders, draughts and ludo.

Looking around, the camp Warden noticed the wet

carpet, covered in sugar, pieces of broken vase, bits of biscuit and broken ornaments and the damaged picture frame.

Guiltily, Dad looked at the campsite Warden and said, 'There's something weird about this caravan.'

'Well, I'm not staying in a filthy caravan like this,' interrupted Mum, not thinking that it was she and her family who had made the mess. 'Come on,' she said, 'we're leaving.'

The whole family packed up their belongings and in no time at all, had driven away with loud grumblings from the grown-ups, moans from the children and the enormous revving of the car engine.

Henry heaved an enormous sigh of relief. In no time at all, the campsite Warden and his wife had cleaned him up and sorted him out.

He was sparkling again, waiting for a nice family to stay with him.

I'm sure he got one, don't you.

Skipper the Kangaroo
has a Lucky Day

It was the hottest summer Skipper could ever remember. It was so hot that the grass and the leaves on the few trees around were shrivelling up. Skipper's Mum and Dad were very worried; the water was drying up too

On this particular day, Skipper was really thirsty.

'I need a drink,' he gasped.

All of his little kangaroo friends were saying the same. The grown up kangaroos had gone off on their own to search for food and Skipper and his friends were lying on the ground among some big rocks

Skipper decided to move further under the largest rock he was resting by.

'There's some shadow here,' cried Skipper. 'It should be cooler here.'

He used his strong hind legs to dig into the shadow but as he dug, the ground suddenly gave way and he found himself falling down into a hole.

'Skipper!' 'Skipper!' shouted his friends as they tumbled down on top of him.

'Ouch! Be careful.' Skipper said as he squeezed out from underneath them.

They all looked around. It seemed to be a cave but not the sort of cave made by under-ground streams. There were some marks on the walls of the cave.

'It's been made by humans,' shouted Skipper.

At one end of the cave they could see a small tunnel, so he decided to explore it.

It did not take long. He soon came back to his friends.

'Come on. It's a lot better in here,' he told them.

A cool draught of air was blowing through the cave. Gratefully, Skipper and his friends crawled along a gloomy passage.

'This is great.'

They weren't scared at all.

After crawling along for some time, the tunnel suddenly opened into another big cave.

Small holes had been cut into the roof of it and bright sunlight shone through them, so that the young kangaroos could see quite well.

Skipper and his friends stretched out on the floor of the cave to have a good rest.

As Skipper lay down, he hit something hard with his head.

'What's that?'

Turning his head, he saw something shiny on the floor. It did not look like an ordinary stone, because it was smooth and when Skipper let the sunlight shining through the hole in the roof fall onto it, it shone with all kinds of different colours.

'It must be a special kind of stone, I'll take it back with me, when we go home,'

He then settled down for a good rest. After a while, they all began to get restless and fidgety.

'I think we'd better get back now otherwise everyone will be worrying about us,'

Skipper said to his friends.

He picked up his 'special stone' and they all made their way back through the tunnel.

When they reached the hole through which they had fallen, Skipper and his friends, with a lot of scrambling, slipping and sliding, managed to climb out into the bright sunshine.

There were a lot of worried-looking mummy and daddy kangaroos wandering about.

'Where have you been?' asked Skipper's Dad.

'Your Mum and I have been very worried about you.'

'Sorry, but look what I've found,'

Skipper's Dad looked at the 'special stone' carefully for a while and then stopped feeling cross.

'Where did you get this?' he asked, quietly.

31

'Inside that big hole I fell into,' replied Skipper.

Looking more closely at the 'stone' Skipper's Dad said, 'I think you have found an opal.'

'An opal! What's that?' asked Skipper excitedly.

His dad explained that it was what humans called a 'precious' stone and they say that it is very valuable.

'I think I've got an idea,' continued Dad, as he called all the other kangaroos together and told them they were all going to visit the human farm in the next valley.

'We need food and water,' he explained to them.

Now on this farm lived an old man who was alone, except for a few chickens and a small herd of cows. He was kind to all animals - even vultures and the crocodiles, which often swam up the river, when it flooded in the spring.

The kangaroos did not know that many of the old man's cows had died in the very hot weather and he was now thinking of leaving the farm and going to town to find other work.

Skipper's Dad did not want to take food and water without giving anything in return - and that's where his idea came in.

The herd of kangaroos were not afraid at all as the old man came out to greet them.'

'Well, what's all this?' asked the old man cheerily.

'We've found this', replied Skipper's Dad, holding out the opal in his big paw.

The old man looked at the opal and his eyes nearly popped out of his head.

'Goodness me,' he said. 'That's the largest opal I've ever seen.'

'Is that so,' replied Skipper's Dad. 'We know that it is valuable to humans and perhaps it could be valuable to us too.'

Skipper's Dad then told the old man about their problem of not finding enough food and water in this very hot weather.

Maybe, in exchange for the opal, they could have what they wanted. That is, food and water, while they all waited until the rains came again, bringing bubbling streams and fresh, green grass.

The old man agreed at once. Now he would be able to keep his farm and buy a new, larger herd of cows.

Skipper and all the kangaroos followed the old man to his windmill, which brought up water from deep underground.

As the windmill began to turn, there was a gurgling sound and water began to fill a trough. Soon everyone had drunk as much water as they all wanted and they all felt much better.

The old man then took a pitchfork, went into the barn and brought out a large bundle of hay.

'There's plenty more when you need it,' he said kindly.

The kangaroos munched away happily and Skipper thought it was the best hay he had ever tasted.'

'You can rest in the barn if you like.' the old man said, adding, 'You may stay as long as you like.'

So Skipper and the rest of the kangaroos went to lie under a huge veranda, next to the barn. The veranda had been built to give shade to the cows in very hot weather.

Skipper and his friends stayed happily by the barn until the rains came again.

He was glad that he had been able to help, though did not realize just how much he had been able to help the old man too.

Bouncy the Elf
and the Goblin Diamonds

One day Bouncy the Elf went for a walk in Fawn Wood. He carried a backpack with a drink and two peanut butter sandwiches. He just wandered about through the wood looking for a quiet spot for a picnic.

He bounced and skipped along the path, singing a little song to himself. He was so busy making up words for a new song that he didn't realize where he was going.

After a while, he suddenly noticed that he had taken a wrong turn and he was in a part of the wood that he didn't know.

Oh, flips, he thought. *I don't want to be out and lost all night. There are all sorts of strange things in this forest. It might be a bit scary.*

He sat down for a minute to have a drink and a sandwich. He took a sip from his bottle of pop and started nibbling at one of his sandwiches.

He was just putting the bottle back into his backpack when he heard a noise.

A clink clink sound.

'What's that?'

Then he heard another strange noise.

35

'Wah! Wah! Wah! Wah!'

Oh no, not Goblins.

Now elves are scared of Goblins because they are usually horrible to them, always bossing them about, often much worse. *So he thought it best to hide behind a big tree.*

Just then he heard another clink. Bouncey carefully looked round the tree trunk and to his amazement saw a long narrow valley.

On the far side of the valley was a steep hill, in which Bouncey saw the entrance to a huge cave. To his surprise, he also saw a set of tiny railway lines coming out of the cave. By the side of the railway lines were piles of shiny rocks.

The railway trucks must have brought them out, he thought.

From inside the cave, the sound of voices, rough sounding voices, which could be heard quite clearly.

Then Bouncey heard that strange clink, clink, sound again 'Oh Flips, it must be one of the Goblin's gold or diamond mines.'

The Elf King had warned all the elves to keep well away from them, because Goblins liked to make many captured elves work like slaves inside their mines, only letting them go when they were too tired to lift up a pick or shovel.

Now quite worried, Bouncey, trying not to make a sound, crawled back along the path he had just been following. When he could hear nothing more, he quickly got to his feet and ran as fast as he could, along the path, towards a small stream he had spied through the trees.

Stopping for a moment to get his breath back, He felt his heart thumping very fast in his chest. Thump! Thump! Thump!

'I must have a rest,' so he sat down by the stream.

He was just reaching for his pop bottle from inside his backpack, when he heard a snorting, snuffling noise from behind his back. Turning around, Bouncey saw a very large, wild boar coming from out of the trees.

The wild boar saw Bouncey and stopped. Two tiny beady eyes, looked out through of a fringe of hair, which fell down across its huge snout. A set of enormous tusks looked even bigger, when the wild boar opened its mouth, wider and wider. It began to grunt and squeal.

Bouncey didn't wait to see to any more. He ran away in terror, not looking back until he could run no further.

It can't get any worse. Can it?

Suddenly, out of the bushes on the other side of the path came two horrible-looking Goblins. They were both carrying sacks and on their belts they each had small hammers and picks, the tools were knocking together making a jingly, jangly sound.

'What are they doing?' Bouncey said to himself.

He watched as the two went across to the other side of the path and pushed aside a large bush, behind it in the hillside, was a cave.

One Goblin pulled two little objects from his sack, a small piece of stone and a lump of metal The other broke off a small bundle of twigs from the bush and put them on the ground and then watched as the other Goblin knocked the stone (it was a piece of flint) and metal together, sparks showered onto the twigs and they soon caught fire.

The other Goblin took from his sack, a ready-made torch. It was just a stick and it had rags tied around the top.

He lit the torch and they both went inside the cave entrance. A few wisps of smoke lingered behind, to show where they had gone.

Bouncy forgot all about being scared and crept nearer the cave and making sure not to step on the burnt twigs, he went inside.

Jingle! Jangle! Jingle!

The sounds got fainter and fainter as the Goblins went further and further into the cave. Bouncy could just see the tiny flame of the torch. So, by keeping the tiny light in sight, he followed the two Goblins down a long tunnel.

Suddenly, it went dark. *Oh flips,* thought Bouncy. *What am I going to do now?*

He put his hands out and touched the sides of the tunnel and slowly carried on until he reached a turning. It was only when he turned round the corner that he could see the torch again.

It had been stuck into a hole in the wall.

The two Goblins had put the sacks down and were using their tools to dig into the sides of the tunnel.

Clink! Clank! Clunk! Clink!

In amongst all the rock and rubble something shone.

'Oh,' gasped Bouncey.

'It's a diamond!'

He now realized he was in one of the Goblin's diamond mines.

The two Goblins started hammering the wall again - another glint:

- then another diamond.

Bouncey watched them for about half an hour.

They found six more diamonds. Then one of the Goblins muttered something to the other, in the strange way that Goblins spoke.

They stopped working and put the diamonds they had found into a sack.

Then one of them pulled the torch out of the hole in the wall. As he did so, some of it fell off and streaked to the ground, burning brightly.

The Goblins ignored it and started walking back along the way they had come, missing Bouncy by centimetres.

Luckily, he had hidden in a hollow next to a pile of small rocks and waited until they had gone.

Bouncy looked over to where the little bit of torch was burning on the piles of rocks and went over and started rummaging amongst them.

'Oh, what's that?' he cried suddenly, and saw two glinting, shining rocks.

'Gosh! Two diamonds.'

So he eagerly bent down and picked them up.

He had just put them into his backpack, when the little bit of burning torch on the ground went out in a puff of smoke.

'Oh Flips. It's so dark. What can I do now?'

He turned slowly around, because he knew if he turned round once, he would be facing the way out. So he put one hand on the wall and edged along the tunnel very slowly and carefully.

On his way out he fell once a few times and banged his head three times. Eventually, he saw the gleam of sunlight at the entrance to the cave, shining through the branches of the large bush.

The Goblins must have gone, he hoped.

He crept to the entrance and looked out.

Yes, across the path, he could see the two Goblins disappearing behind the tree where he had hidden, ages before.

He waited a bit longer and crept out. He then walked onto the path and ran as fast as he could, deciding along the way, that if he went downhill he might get to a stream that flowed into the river that went by the Elf village.

Just as luck would have it, that's exactly what happened.

He ran down and there was a stream. He followed the stream and came to the river that went all the way down to his village.

He was out of breath by now and as he rushed into the Elf village. One of the Kings' of the Elves guards asked sternly. 'Where have you been?'

Now, Elves are well cared for and they have to tell the guards where they are going if they ever have to go out of the Elf village.

If they are away too long everyone gets worried about them - even the King.

'Just for a walk,' gasped Bouncy, breathlessly.

'Well the Kings wants to see you,' the chief guard told

him and they took him along to the Palace of the Elf King.

The King was glad to see Bouncy but was also a little cross. 'Now then, Bouncy.' said the Elf King sternly.

'Where have you been? I've not seen you for ages.

'I ...I... foun..found and.. Gob..Gob..Gobl...rail.. rail... wild...wild.

He was so excited that he hardly knew what he was saying. Taking a deep breath, Bouncey said, 'I've found a Goblin diamond mine. Your majesty!'

Bouncy then put his hand into his backpack and pulled out the two diamonds. 'They're presents for you,' your Majesty

'Oh, thank you! Bouncy' said the Elf King with a big smile. 'That's wonderful - but keep one for yourself. You deserve it for all your efforts of today.'

Then, rubbing his hands together in excitement the Elf King said, 'Can you draw me a plan or map so that we can go back to the mine?'

The Elf King looked carefully at Bouncey, his eyes shining, waiting for his answer.

Bouncy thought and thought. 'Well, there's the River of Dreams and the stream to follow - Oh flips' said Bouncey. 'I'm not too sure. There are lots and lots of streams that go into our river. I'll never remember where it is,' apologized Bouncey.

'Well never mind,' said the disappointed Elf King. 'You've done very well - now go to the Royal Kitchen and you can pick whatever you like.'

What do you think Bouncey had?

Actually, it was a bun with white icing and a big red cherry on the top, a chocolate covered ice-lolly, a glass of a fizzy fruit smoothie and a great big super ice - cream cornet.

They were delicious!

Bouncy never could decide which was the right stream to follow.

He still dreams of finding the diamond mine again and perhaps one day he will

Peta the Plane
and the Lost Little Girl

Peta the Plane was on the runway and the Pilot was giving him his last polish before take off. The smoother his wings, the faster he could fly.

'I'm ready to go,' said Peta to the Pilot.

'Hang on Peta - I'll just go and see where we are going for our next trip,' replied the Pilot.

As the pilot walked towards the control tower, Peta started up the engine. It was running nicely when the Pilot came rushing out.

'Peta! Peta!' he shouted excitedly.

'A little girl has been very silly and has taken her inflatable boat out alone. Now she is lost. Her Mum and Dad are very worried.'

'We've been asked to go and see if we can find her.' added the Pilot.

'Let's go then,' cried Peta.

Taking off as quickly as he could, Peta, zoomed into the air. He flew over the beach and towards Seal Island.

Going at top speed, it wasn't long before the Island came into view.

Peta zoomed down to the beach.

It was high tide, so there was no sand to be seen. On top of the high cliffs, a few sheep wandered about and screeching seagulls circled in the air.

There was no sign of the girl on the bare cliff tops or beyond, where only short, scrubby grass grew.

We'll have to try the mountains,' said the Pilot.

'Okay,' replied Peta.

43

Peta zoomed down towards the mountains. They soon
reached the highest mountain and circled around it.

'Can you get any lower Peta?' asked the Pilot.

'I'll try,' said Peta. 'These mountains are very high and
if I go too low the winds might blow me onto them.'

'Well, do your best.'

Peta flew nearer and nearer the tall mountain peaks.

They circled around three peaks, as low as he could but there was no sign of the girl. All they saw were some wild horses on the lower slopes and what looked like a big, brown bear among some trees.

'Oh!' exclaimed Peta. 'I can't imagine the little girl getting up here. Can you?'

'You never know,' replied the Pilot.

'If she was exploring she might not have realized how far she had gone. We'd better try the lake area now.'

So Peta flew down to the bottom of the mountains. There was the big lake - very deep - very dark and looking very, very mysterious. A small river flowed from it to the sea. In the middle of the lake was a small island and as Peta flew nearer to it, the Pilot called out excitedly.'

'Look. Peta. Look There's something down there.'

Peta flew lower and skimmed over the lake towards the island. Sure enough, as they went nearer, they could see some sort of shelter made with branches. Just in front of the shelter, they could see a little white face and a hand waving. A small inflatable boat lay nearby.

Peta circled lower and lower. They could see the girl now. She was only nine years old they had been told and she looked as though she was hurt.

She was lying down, resting on one arm, waving weakly.

'I bet she's starving hungry,' said Peta. 'What are we going to do?'

'We've got a problem haven't we?' replied the Pilot. 'You've got wheels so you can't land on the lake. But I have an idea. First we'll drop some emergency supplies.'

The Pilot took the emergency pack out. It contained first aid equipment, food and water.

When it was dropped from a plane a little parachute opened out, floating the package down safely.

The pilot tied a little note to the package telling the girl not to worry and they would be back soon.

'Fly down the far side of the Island so I can drop the package,' ordered the Pilot.

Peta zoomed down. He went in as low as he dared making sure not to stall his engine and maybe crash.

The Pilot then leaned out of the cockpit window and dropped the package, pulling a string as he did so. The parachute opened out and fortunately landed a few metres from the girl.

They saw her crawl to the package and give a wave. The Pilot waved back.

'Let's get back to the airport as quickly as we can,' instructed the Pilot.

Peta flew off at top speed. As he did so, the Pilot radioed the airport and gave certain instructions to the control tower.

'What did you say?' asked Peta.

'You'll soon find out,' replied the Pilot with a smile.

As soon as they got close to the airport, Peta noticed quite a lot of activity. There was a lorry parked next to where he was going to land and certain objects lay on the ground next to the it.

'What's going on?' asked Peta curiously.

'We're going to try to put floats on your wheels so you can land in the water,' replied the Pilot.

Peta was very excited. Not long after he landed, workmen brought some pieces of wood along with some plastic tubing and began fixing them to his wheels. They were like skis to start with - the plastic tubing would keep him float.

The floats were strapped and screwed on, just high enough for Peta to use his wheels as well.

Soon Peta was ready and took off for Seal Island at top speed. Once more the island came into view.

'Now, remember you're not used to landing on water,' the Pilot reminded Peta.

Peta waggled his wings, he knew he had to be very careful and he circled once, then went towards one end of the lake and touched down on the water.

Splash!

Water sprayed out all over Peta.

'It might stop my engine,' cried Peta in an alarmed voice.

So he turned the engine speed down and they slowly floated to the edge of the island where the girl's camp was.

The girl was lying in her shelter. They could hear her faint cries of, 'Help! Over here!'

The Pilot took out a rope and attached it to Peta's wheel-strut and waded through the shallow water to tie the other end to a nearby tree. Then he went quickly up to the girl.

'Oh! I'm so glad you've come,' said the girl in a weak little voice.

The girl had hurt her leg, so the Pilot picked her up very carefully.

'Oh! Oh! OH! OOOHHH!' cried the little girl.

'I'm sorry' said the Pilot, 'but I've got to get you to the plane.'

The little girl was very brave as the Pilot waded through the water, opened Peta's door and placed her carefully in the back seat, before buckling her in securely. He then untied the rope attached to the tree and the wheel and got into the cabin.

'Now be careful taking off,' warned the Pilot to Peta.

'Remember you're not a real sea plane.'

Peta started the engine and began the longest run he could make - from one end of the lake to the other.

Spray splashed everywhere - even over the windscreen. The Pilot could hardly see.

Peta almost panicked. 'The engine's going to flood! The engine's going to flood!' he wailed.

48

'Just keep going,' shouted the Pilot over the noise of the whirring engine and the crashing spray. 'You'll be OK.'

The end of the lake came into view and Peta just managed to take off, water dripping onto the trees below.

They heard the little girl moaning quietly, so Peta went at top speed and they soon arrived back at the airport, where a large crowd was waiting.

The ambulance had already arrived and the ambulance men placed the little girl carefully onto a stretcher.

The little girl's mum and Dad were also waiting by the Control Tower.

They were going to the hospital too of course but they wanted to thank Peta and the Pilot first.

With it's siren blaring and lights flashing the ambulance rushed the little girl away to hospital.

'Well done Peta,' said the Pilot a little while later, as he patted his wing.

'Just glad I could help,' replied Peta with a huge smile, as everyone clapped.

Bouncey the Elf
Meets a Wizard

It was a lovely sunny day, so Bouncey the Elf decided to go for a walk. He went to find his backpack and put in a bottle of pop and a pack of biscuits.

He then set off into the forest with a bouncy walk, along the banks of the River of Dreams, singing a song to himself.

He was just wandered around when he saw a blue and red bird he had never seen before. It seemed very tame.

Suddenly, Bouncey heard a grunting sound in the bushes. It was a wild boar.

Bouncey was not scared, just curious, so he began to follow it.

The wild boar went here, there and everywhere. This way and that way, up tracks Bouncey had never seen before. He was really enjoying himself - until he realized he was lost.

'Oh no!' he said in a worried voice. 'It always happens to me.'

He was standing still, wondering what to do next, when he heard a strange noise - a whooshing - sound.

He looked up the path, and saw a big hill and what appeared to be the entrance of a cave. So he crept slowly towards it.

Bending low, he crept towards a big rock resting by a big tree and keeping as quiet as he could, looked into the cave and saw the strangest person.

He was tall, dressed in long dark robes with a tall pointed hat, patterned with stars. He had a long, straggling grey beard, pointed nose and crooked fingers, which held a wand over a bubbling cauldron.

'This must be the Wizard's cave,' Bouncey said excitedly to himself.

The Wizard then started to wave his wand again and - whoosh - a big puff of smoke came from the cauldron.

Kneeling behind the rock opposite to the entrance to the cave, he watched curiously as the Wizard threw something into it.

Then sparks from the fire flew out all over the cave - some of them even found their way to the entrance, not far from where Bouncey was hiding.

He moved away hurriedly to avoid some of them.

The Wizard noticed his movement. 'Who's there?' he called out sharply, looking round with glaring eyes.

Then he pointed towards Bouncey with a bony finger. 'Come here,' he said in a stern voice.

Bouncey crept forward, shivering with fright.

'Who are you?' The Wizard asked loudly.

'I - I - I'm Bouncey the Elf,' stuttered poor Bouncey.

'Why are you spying on me,' demanded the Wizard. 'I usually turn spies into frogs or toads.'

'I wasn't spying - honest,' protested Bouncy in a trembling voice.

'I just came upon you by accident and was curious - please don't turn me into a frog.'

'Go and sit over there. I'll deal with you in a minute,' ordered the Wizard.

He pointed to a stool in the far corner of the cave.

Bouncey went and sat down, wishing all the time he had acted more sensibly and not played chasing games with a wild boar.

The Wizard waved his wand over the cauldron again - there was another - whoosh - smoke and more sparks.

'Good - that's finished now,' said the Wizard, taking the cauldron off the fire.

He turned to Bouncey.

'I won't be long. Don't touch anything.'

There was a little door at the back of the cave and the Wizard went through to the next room.

Bouncey looked around the cave.

It was full of jars - stacked on stone shelves carved into the rock. Inside the jars were things like bat's wings and snake's eyes - lots of the most horrible things you can imagine.

He was too scared to move.

The Wizard soon came back with a little jug in his hand and dipped it into the bubbling cauldron and filled it.

Lifting the jug to his mouth he took a sip – and immediately disappeared.

Bouncey couldn't believe his eyes

There was a chuckle and with a snap of fingers, the Wizard reappeared.

'That's marvelous!' cried Bouncey, forgetting his terror.

'Oh! Just one of my little spells,' said the Wizard, a little more kindly.

'I'm going to a Wizard's party and this is what I'll be taking.'

'Is it far away?' asked Bouncey.

'It will take me a good week travelling on my magic carpet' answered the Wizard.

Bouncey's eyes opened even wider at the other mention of a magic carpet

By now the Wizard seemed quite friendly and he asked Bouncey if he would like something to eat.

He left the little jug on the table, went out to the room and came back with a delicious-looking piece of chocolate cake and a glass of ginger beer.

'Here you are,' said the Wizard.

'It's been quite nice to have some company. It gets a little lonely here sometimes,' he said sadly.

Then the Wizard smiled and said.

'I don't really change people into frogs and toads you know.'

Bouncey gave a nervous little laugh and then relaxed and enjoyed his cake and ginger beer.

'I'd better be off now.'

The Wizard looked over at his pet owl, which had just given two loud hoots.

He took out a key and locked the little door at the back of the cave. Then he poured the now cooled contents of the cauldron into a green jar and jammed in the stopper.

The Wizard slowly walked to the entrance of the cave and snapped his fingers three times.

The carpet that Bouncey was standing on suddenly started to move.

'Wow.'

He jumped off quickly, just managing not to fall over.
The magic carpet moved towards the Wizard, who sat
down on it and put his magic brew into a bag

'Sorry I can't stop, it's been nice meeting you but duty calls.' And he pulled his tall hat tight over his ears.

'Bye for now, Bouncey,' shouted the Wizard, as he and the magic carpet, started flying out of the cave.

Higher and higher they went, until they were over the treetops and out of sight.

Bouncey was just about to go himself, when he noticed the little jug on the table.

I'm sure the Wizard won't mind me taking a little drop, thought Bouncey.

So he emptied his water bottle outside the cave and then went back and poured some of the magic mixture into it.

Then he walked out into the sunshine with a bouncy step and tried to find his way home.

After wandering around for a time, he was lucky enough to find a path he knew and was soon back at the Elf Village.

He was trying to creep through the palace gates when two guards noticed him.

'Come with us, Bouncey - the Elf King wants to see you.'

So Bouncey went to see the Elf King, who said sternly. 'You have been on one of your walks again without telling anyone - haven't you?'

'Well, your Majesty, I found the Wizard's cave.' announced Bouncey proudly.

'What do you mean?' exclaimed the Elf King.

'Nobody can go in there without coming out as a frog or toad.'

'It was alright, really,' said Bouncey. He then told the Elf King everything what had happened to him that day

Then he took out his water bottle. Unfortunately, he hadn't screwed the top on tightly enough. It had spilled out and there was only one drop left in the bottle.

Bouncey took a sip and disappeared

The Elf King was amazed. 'Where are you?'

'I'm here your Majesty,' replied Bouncey from across the room.

'Where?' asked the Elf King again, looking around the room and not seeing Bouncey.

'Here,' laughed Bouncey who was standing behind the Elf King.

'Stop playing around, Bouncey' ordered the Elf King in an angry voice.

So Bouncey clicked his fingers twice and re-appeared.

He then had to tell the Elf King there was no more magic mixture left.

'Oh dear, what fun I could have had with that,' sighed the Elf King.

'Never mind Bouncey, as a reward, you can go to the royal kitchens and ask for whatever you wish.'

So Bouncey rushed down to the royal kitchens and asked for -

a huge fresh cream chocolate éclair - a drink of fizzy apple juice and then a giant chocolate ice - cream cornet.

Bouncey, when he's in the forest, often looks up, hoping to catch a glimpse of the magic flying carpet and the friendly Wizard

Perhaps, one day, he will.

Eddy the Lifeboat
and the Lighthouse Keeper

Eddy was really pleased. He was being cleaned extra carefully because there was going to be an inspection of the Lifeboat Station. This was an inspection to find the most, well - kept lifeboat in the whole country.

Eddy had been runner-up twice before but he had never won first prize. The lifeboat crew were busy cleaning the portholes, brass fittings and the engine had been polished until it shone. Eddy was really sparkling and everyone thought he had a good chance of being the number one lifeboat.

The Captain was smiling with pleasure, sure that Eddy would do very well.

Suddenly the telephone rang. It was the Coastguard Station with an emergency call.

A lighthouse keeper on Seal Island has slipped on a rock and has broken his arm –

Can you help?

They asked, hopefully if Eddy the Lifeboat could help with the rescue because it was too windy for a rescue helicopter.

'We can go now,' said the Captain. 'Can't we, Eddy?'

'Yes we can, as soon as the crew get to action stations.' replied Eddy.

The Captain immediately pressed Eddy's alarm button. His siren nearly deafened everyone on the Lifeboat and the crew rushed for their wet- weather clothes and were soon ready to take Eddy to sea.

A sailor then used a hammer to knock a spike out of a chain that kept Eddy from sliding down into the sea. Clink! - Clank! - Bang!

Slowly at first, then faster and faster, Eddy slid down the ramp and entered with a big splash into the water.

'Now then Eddy,' ordered the Captain. 'Top speed please, the lighthouse keeper must be in a lot of pain with his broken arm.'

So Eddy raced off through the sea as fast as his engines would let him. The strong winds that had prevented the helicopter from rescuing the injured lighthouse - keeper, were making very big waves. He was having some difficulty getting through the huge waves. He was bobbing up and bobbing down.

Up, up, urrrpp and downnnnn. Up, up, urrrpp and downnnnn.

'Ooooer, I don't like this,' cried Eddy as another giant wave swooped down at him. He went down into the waves as they smashed over the front of him with a loud boom. The sea then rushed over his nice clean deck, again and again.

'Oh no, I've just remembered,' cried Eddy.

'The Inspection's tomorrow, I'll not stand a chance now.'

'You're here to save lives, not for winning competitions,' replied the Captain with a smile.

'I know,' said Eddy sorrowfully. 'Although it would be nice to win at least once.'

'The crew will be disappointed too,' went on the Captain. 'They worked very hard getting you ready.'

Eddy the Lifeboat soon stopped feeling sorry for himself and concentrated on going up and down through the giant waves.

Suddenly, one of the crew shouted out.

'Captain!'

'Eddy!'

'LOOK. LOOK!'

There, floating right in front of Eddy was a huge tree. 'Hard astern Eddy, quickly now,' shouted the Captain.

For just a moment, Eddy the Lifeboat thought he might not be able to slow down quickly enough. Then, with a mighty roar, his engines began to spin his propellers backwards.

Just in time, Eddy began to slow down missing the tree by a few centimeters. Then, as the giant tree began to slide along the side of Eddy, the Captain suddenly cried out.

'Just look at that!'

Clinging tightly to one of the topmost branches of the tree was a tiny kitten.

'We have to save the little kitten before it drowns,' shouted Eddy.

'Yes,' agreed the Captain, as he ordered a sailor to tie a rope to the giant tree.

Quickly, before the sea could pull them apart, another sailor jumped onto the floating tree and climbed up to the frightened kitten.

The giant tree was beginning to pull away, the rope stretching to breaking point.

'Jump,' shouted Eddy to the sailor holding the little kitten.

Carefully putting the little kitten inside his coat, the sailor jumped down onto the deck, just as the rope holding the giant tree snapped in two.

'My! That was close.' said Eddy with relief.

'Take the kitten down to the galley (kitchen), for some

milk,' ordered the Captain to the brave sailor who had made the rescue.

After another hour and a half of going through more rough seas, Eddy managed to get to Seal Island.

The sea was smashing against the rocks, with a great roaring sound and spray showering into the air.

This is going to be awkward, thought Eddy.

At the end of the Island was a huge rock and it was on this that the lighthouse was built.

The job of the two lighthouse keepers was to make sure that the light shone every night to warn ships to keep their distance from the dangerous rocks.'

'Let's see how close you can get, Eddy.' said the Captain in a worried voice.

Eddy slowed his engine down and steadily chugged along, rising up and down in the rough sea. Just by using the two propellers - one forwards and one backwards, he could remain in the same place. Although he did bob up and down alarmingly in the huge swell.

Everyone stared at the waves crashing down on the rocks at the bottom of the lighthouse.

'We'll never be able to get a boat in there,' said the Captain to the crew.

'We'll have to use a *Breeches Buoy.*'

'What's that?' asked Eddy.

'Well, we have to send up a rope to the top of the lighthouse and then haul up the '*Breeches Buoy.*' It's just a special seat you pull up on a rope,' replied the Captain, as he set about getting everything ready. He then spoke on the radiophone to tell the two lighthouse keepers of his plan.

Quickly, one of the sailors picked up a big crossbow. They waited until they could see one of the lighthouse keepers waving at the top of the lighthouse.

'Now,' shouted the Captain. 'Fire!'

'Twangggg!!!' The huge arrow from the crossbow, with a thin rope attached, was caught in a huge gust of wind and fell back into the sea.

'Try again,' ordered the Captain. When the arrow and line had been pulled, dripping wet from the sea. The sailor refitted it to the crossbow and fired again.

'Twanggg!!!' This time it went straight up towards the top of the lighthouse and caught on a railing. The lighthouse keeper quickly grabbed it and tied the end securely onto the railing of the lighthouse and began to pull up the line connected to the *Breeches Buoy*.

A sailor sat inside it. It would need two men to deal with the injured lighthouse keeper. Carefully, the sailor was slowly pulled up to the top of the lighthouse.

Meanwhile, Eddy was still struggling in the giant waves. When the sailor reached the top of the lighthouse everyone gave a great cheer, as he stepped out of his special seat. He and the lighthouse keeper then went into the lighthouse.

Soon, three figures could be seen, one of them with a sling over his arm. The two men, very carefully, helped the injured man into the special seat and he was soon safely lowered down to Eddy the Lifeboat. Luckily, just before a huge wave swept past them.

The special seat was sent back to collect the other sailor who was soon safely aboard the Eddy.

The remaining lighthouse keeper gave a wave and then went to the radiophone to give his thanks and ask them to keep him informed about his injured friend.

The Captain then called to Eddy. 'Back we go - slowly now!'

The sea seemed even rougher as Eddy began his return journey. The wind howled and the waves crashed over his deck even more fiercely.

What a journey it was. Eddy struggled to keep the boat upright, thinking of the poor lighthouse keeper with his injured arm.

When they eventually arrived at the Lifeboat Station, there was an ambulance waiting to rush the injured man to hospital.

The Captain decided he would take the rescued kitten home for one of his grandchildren.

Eddy was then towed up the ramp and the chain locked in place with the big metal spike.

Clang!

Eddy was now safely back at the Lifeboat Station.

'Well, Eddy, that was a job well done,' said the Captain cheerfully.

Eddy, who was only thinking of the next day's inspection and was feeling upset, said nothing.

The following morning the Inspector arrived. He had

heard all about the emergency trip so, looking at Eddy the Lifeboat, he said, 'I heard you did a great job yesterday and I'm sorry I can't give you a certificate for being the cleanest and most well maintained lifeboat.'

'However, I have got a special award for you, the Captain and crew for being so brave in those rough seas.'

He then unrolled a beautifully framed Certificate for Bravery.

Eddy the Lifeboat, the Captain and the crew had never felt so proud.

Aerie the Faery
and the Unicorn

Aerie was a fairy who did not fit in very well with her many friends. For a start she did not like her long golden hair. Everyone kept saying how beautiful she looked when the wind blew her hair into long streamers around her pretty face.

The problem was that Aerie wanted to go exploring, to visit dangerous places like Wild Boar Forest just like one of her friends Bouncey the Elf did.

Aerie knew that her long hair would soon become tangled and caught if she tried to pass through the thick bushes and low branches of the forest.

Of course, Aerie knew she could wear a hat but that wouldn't work. She hated hats.

Years ago, when she was very small, her mother had made her a special hat. It was shaped like a giant strawberry, bright red with a long green stalk sticking right up into the air.

When Aerie went outside to play with her friends they all started to laugh. She did not know that a blackbird had perched on the top of her hat and was pecking at what it thought was a giant strawberry. Aerie squealed when she realized that a bird was on her head, pecking her hat.

'Get it off me' she shouted. Her friends laughed all the more loudly.

So Aerie ran back home, sobbing and crying for her mother to take off her new hat. The blackbird had of course, already flown off.

From that day Aerie had never worn another hat.

It was a nice sunny morning when Aerie got her idea. Quickly dressing and without any breakfast, she walked through the fairy village without stopping or speaking to any of her friends.

Outside the fairy village was a large cave, the home of a white witch who was a good friend of Aerie's.

'Can you please help me?' Aerie asked the White Witch. 'I need someone to cut my hair, very short.'

'Oh! I couldn't do that.' replied the White Witch. 'Cut your lovely hair. Oh no.'

'Tell me though, Aerie, why do you want me to cut your hair.'

'Well,' said Aerie.

Then she told the White Witch all about wanting to go exploring and that her long hair would be a problem when going through the forest.

'I see.' said the White Witch quietly. 'Maybe I can help you but in another way.'

Going to a nearby cupboard, the White Witch picked up one of her special magic brews. It was in a small brown bottle.

'Just rub a few drops of this into your hair but make sure you keep your eyes tightly closed.'

'What will it do?' asked Aerie, feeling a little alarmed.

'Don't worry.' replied the White Witch. 'It will shrink your hair so short that you will not be troubled travelling through the thick forest trees and bushes.'

'What,' cried Aerie. 'Lose all my hair with a magic spell.'

'Don't worry,' said the White Witch. 'To get your hair back, all you have to do is wash your head with twenty drops of morning dew.'

'Great,' said Aerie. 'I'll do it.' Thanking the White Witch, Aerie went back home to pack for her trip into Wild Boar Forest.

Very early the next morning Aerie opened the magic bottle and rubbed seven drops of the magic mixture into her lovely long hair.

One. Two. Three minutes went by then Aerie felt a strange tingling in her head.

WHOOSH!

Her long golden hair had gone.

'Oh my,' said a startled Aerie. She looked into her mirror and saw that her hair was now just like a furry covering on the top of her head.

Quickly getting over her surprise. She wrote a note to her parents saying that she was going away for a few days and they were not to worry.

Now Aerie had often heard about many of her friend Bouncey the Elf's adventures and of how he always took food and drinks whenever he went on a trip. So she made sure that she did the same.

Although Aerie, like all other fairies, had wings, she didn't use them all the time. So making sure that the straps of her backpack did not snag her wings, she set off for Wild Boar Forest.

The journey took her towards the Village of the Elves. Nearby, a path led her through Fawn Wood and to the bridge over the River of Dreams.

Crossing the bridge, Aerie could see in the distance the dark gloomy trees of Wild Boar forest.

Aerie suddenly felt a little scared. So she stopped for a moment.

I bet Bouncey the Elf didn't feel scared she thought to herself. *So neither will I.*

Walking on through some thick bushes, Aerie was glad she had got rid of her long hair. It really was much easier with short hair and she did not need a horrible hat.

By now Aerie was getting rather warm and just a little tired. 'I need a drink and a rest,' she said to herself.

Sitting by a small stream, Aerie opened her backpack and had a drink from one of her six-pack cokes, carefully replacing the empty can.

Still feeling quite tired, Aerie lay back in the grass and closed her eyes. *Emmm, that's nice,* she thought.

Suddenly she heard a snuffling noise from behind some bushes. Turning around, Aerie saw a very large wild boar coming from out of the trees.

Tiny beady eyes looked out through a fringe of hair, which fell down across its huge snout. A set of enormous tusks could be seen as the wild boar opened its mouth wider and wider. It grunted loudly. Then the wild boar saw Aerie and stopped. It began to paw the ground, still snuffling and grunting,

Aerie quickly sat up and grabbed her backpack in one hand and pushed herself upright with the other one. Now she could use her wings.

Flip. Flap. – Flip. Flap. – Flip. Flap, Aerie rose up off the ground. Flying right over the startled wild boar, she gave great big shout. 'Yeeeeeeeee!'

The wild boar looked up, squealed and ran away.

Aerie flew for a several hundred metres and then landed softly in a glade full of brightly coloured flowers. 'Phew! That was close.' she said to herself.

One of the problems of Wild Boar Forest was the fact that Goblins sometimes went into it to hunt for the secretive, harmless unicorns.

Fortunately, Goblins as well as being horrible and nasty creatures are very noisy and no one has ever heard of them catching a unicorn.

So Aerie still had to be extra careful as she continued to explore Wild Boar Forest. After a while she thought it must be lunchtime, so Aerie looked for a nice place to eat her meal.

Soon she found what looked like a good spot. A hill, with a small stream gushing merrily out of a cave towards a sparkling pool

'Ooo! I could just do with a swim,' said Aerie eagerly.

Two ticks later she was in the pool, splashing and giggling to herself. Aerie was very pleased with her exploration of Wild Boar Forest.

Then she heard a horrible noise. It sounded like a pony that had hurt itself and the noise was coming from inside the cave.

Drying herself quickly with the towel she had fortunately put into her backpack, Aerie carefully went inside the cave.

There was just room for a little track beside the bubbling stream for her to walk along. Further in, the cave became darker but Aerie could just see were she was going.

In the gloom she could see the outline of a small horse or pony. It lay on its side with a big rope tied cruelly round its neck holding it down to the cave floor.

Before Aerie could do anything, a horrible looking Goblin appeared from the other end of the cave. It was the hairiest Goblin Aerie had ever seen. It was disgusting. Its hair hung down, greasy and grimy all the way to the floor.

The Goblin sat down by the little horse and poked it with his horrible foot. The little horse gave a little whinny and the Goblin laughed.

'That does it,' said Aerie to herself. 'That Goblin's for it now. How could it do that to a poor helpless horse.'

A short time later, the Goblin got up and picked up a few sticks from the cave floor and began to make a fire.

Oh no, Aerie nearly called out aloud. There in the firelight was a little unicorn, not a horse or pony.

How can I rescue the unicorn from this horrible Goblin?

73

Thinking hard, Aerie clapped her tiny hands together. 'Yes,' she whispered happily. 'It might work.'

Hoping she had brought it. Aerie looked inside her backpack, fingers crossed. Yes, there it was, the little brown bottle the White Witch had given her yesterday. Would the magic mixture work on the Goblin?

Keeping as quiet as she could, Aerie crept towards the sleeping Goblin, the little brown bottle held out before her.

Holding the magic mixture above the Goblin's head, Aerie shook the brown bottle and several large drops splashed down onto the Goblin's filthy, grimy hair. He gave a loud moan and then turned over, still asleep.

Three minutes later, the Goblin gave a loud cry, and sat up rubbing his head. A large tuft of hair fell to the floor of the cave. As he looked at it, more and more hair fell to the floor and the Goblin started to shake and shiver.

'My hair,' he shrieked. By now all of his hair had gone. 'They won't let me back into the Goblins' Lair,' he moaned and then cried out. 'What can I do?'

Saying that he rushed out to the cave entrance, never to be seen again.

'Oh dear! I must have given him too much of the magic mixture,' said Aerie. 'Still, he did deserve it for hurting the little unicorn.'

'Oh my! The little unicorn,' cried Aerie rushing over to where it lay. As quickly as she could, she untied the rope that was holding the unicorn down. Then slowly and very carefully Aerie led it to the pool by the cave mouth.

The little unicorn was very thirsty and it drank and drank until Aerie thought there wouldn't be enough water in the pool.

Wandering what to do next, Aerie took out her towel and began to rub the little unicorn dry, because it had splashed itself quite a lot when it first went into the pool.

As Aerie rubbed the tiny horn of the little unicorn dry, a small cloud suddenly appeared and a voice spoke from within it.

'Aerie! Do not be afraid. I am Athan, Keeper of the Unicorns. I wish to thank you for saving one of my unicorns. It is too young to know what you have done for it.'

'However! Whenever you are near Mirror Lake, in the Barren Mountains, keep this day in your memory and you will be rewarded.'

'But for now wear this. Thank you and farewell.'

The cloud then disappeared, as did the little unicorn.

Aerie noticed a beautiful wreath of flowers by the cave pool. Picking it up she thought it reminded her of a hat, so she put it on without thinking.

In blink of an eye Aerie was back home, just by the front gate and it was early in the morning she noticed. Remembering what the White Witch had told her, she picked twenty buttercups, each one holding a drop of morning dew.

Quickly, Aerie squeezed each drop onto her head. That strange feeling of tingling and then - her long flowing golden locks were back. She felt much better now. Maybe she had been too keen to have short hair.

I mean, she thought, *exploring Wild Boar forest was all right but now that she had done it, the urge to go back wasn't there. What did Athan mean about Mirror Lake? Now I wonder if that golden ribbon is still in my trinket box, it would really go with my hair.*

Strangely, no one seems to have noticed that she had been away.

Another thing. Aerie always liked to wear hats from that day onwards.

Bouncey the Elf
and the
Spiders Silken Thread

It was a scorching hot day and Bouncey the Elf was having a swim in the River of Dreams, trying to keep cool. Closing his eyes, he took a deep breath and dived under the water, his legs kicking and splashing. When he opened his eyes Bouncey saw that the bottom of the river was covered with smooth pebbles and fronds of river grass, which seemed to wave to him as he swam by them.

As Bouncey glided along the river bottom, a group of green and yellow striped fish darted into the fronds of river grass and a shy crayfish scuttled away into a dark opening of an underwater cave.

Quickly rising to the surface of the river for a breath of fresh air, he then dived down and swam into the underwater cave to follow the crayfish.

It went dark very quickly and Bouncey lost sight of the crayfish and then he had a thought that maybe he had been a little reckless.

So, feeling his way very carefully by touching the slimy walls of the underwater cave, Bouncey went in, deeper and deeper until he felt the pebbly floor of the cave suddenly hit his knees.

Looking up, he saw a shiny patch of light reflecting in the water.

So, just in time, Bouncey poked his head above the water and took a big, big breath.

'Oooh! That's better,' he said, his voice echoing round the pool that he had just emerged into.

The pool was inside a large cave, about 25 metres wide and he could see because hanging from the roof of the cave were several clumps of a glowing fungus.

'Wow,' cried Bouncey looking around the cave.

On the edge of the pool he saw leaning against the wall two spears and a large fishing net drying on the cave floor. A basket made out of strange looking material lay next to the net.

'Wow,' said Bouncey again as he climbed out of the pool, disturbing a shoal of green and yellow striped fish as he did so.

Standing up, Bouncey shivered. 'Oooh! It's cold in here'. He was only wearing his swimming trunks and shivering again he decided to look inside the basket.

It contained, Bouncey saw, a pile of odds and ends. A shell tied to a piece of string, a box full of wriggling grubs, a tangled fishing line but best of all a grey coloured tunic rolled up amongst all the other stuff.

The tunic, smelling of fish of course, was big enough to fit Bouncey. So feeling much warmer after he had put it on he looked for a way out of the cave.

Walking by the two spears Bouncey saw the entrance to a small tunnel, which also had clumps of the glowing fungus hanging in it.

Not knowing what to expect, he crept slowly along the narrow tunnel.

After a while he heard a sort of clicking, scratching noise.

Bouncey stopped and listened and then, creeping round a bend in the tunnel, he gave a loud gasp. 'Oh no, spiders.'

He could see lots and lots of large hairy spiders.

They were everywhere, hanging down from the roof of the tunnel on long spiders threads. Some were running in a horrible scuttling way. Up and down walls, each one leaving a long thin strand of silken web thread.

Suddenly there was a loud bang.

Looking along the tunnel Bouncey saw that a large section of the wall had opened like a door and two strange figures came out.

They were quite small with long thin arms and tiny legs. Their eyes, in big heads, were large with black slits just like a cat.

Each figure was dressed in a dark grey tunic, just like the one Bouncey was wearing. They were pulling a cart made of a dark grey material, with tiny wheels made out of stiffened pieces of the same stuff towards a pile of silken balls of web thread.

Without seeming to notice the spiders, the two figures silently and quickly filled their cart with the balls of silken thread and began to pull it towards the opening in the wall.

'Wait for me,' shouted Bouncey just as the door in the wall began to close.

The two figures stopped pulling the cart and turned towards Bouncey. They just looked, saying nothing. Then Bouncey noticed that one of the figures was blinking his large eyes very quickly.

'Who are you?' A picture came inside Bouncey's head of someone talking.

'What are you doing here? It is not allowed.'

'Flips,' said an amazed Bouncey.

'Are you the Piccs?'

The Piccs are a secret people few have heard of, let alone seen. They speak and 'talk' to each other by thinking what they want to say. You can tell if they are 'talking' because their large eyes blink quickly.

'Yes,' one of them blinked.

'You can't stay here, you must go away.'

'Well, my name is Bouncey the Elf and I don't know the way back. I'm lost,' he told them.

The two Piccs looked at each other and then waved at Bouncey.

'Follow us,' they blinked.

So Bouncey followed them and the slowly moving cart along the new tunnel. The glowing fungus lit the tunnel very well and before long they reached a large cavern.

The two Piccs unloaded the balls of silken spiders thread. Then they pointed down the cavern to a large hut. 'Go there,' they blinked at him.

Walking along a pathway towards the large hut, Bouncey heard a loud scream. He ran as fast as he could in his bare feet (he had no time to put shoes on) towards it. *Who could that be,* he thought. *The Piccs don't make any sounds.*

When he reached the hut, Bouncey was surprised to see a large crowd of Piccs in front of the doorway. Lying on the floor was a small person, crying in pain.

'Oh my,' said Bouncey, 'It's Trixie the Pixie. Is she badly hurt?' One of the Piccs turned and blinked. 'She has a big bump on her head as well as a twisted ankle and cannot walk.'

'Who did it?' demanded Bouncey in a worried voice. 'Trixie is a good friend of mine.'

'We think it is the Goblins,' blinked the Picc.

'We found her lying in a new hole in the tunnel wall not far from here.'

'Why would the Goblins do that?'

'They are our enemies,' blinked the Picc.

'The Goblins want all of the spiders silken thread for themselves. It is very valuable.'

'The spiders thread is so strong and it can be used in many different ways.'

Blinking fast, the Picc added, 'Look at your tunic and you saw the cart. Both are made from our spiders' special silken thread.'

'I see', said Bouncey. 'The Goblins want to steal your store of spiders silken thread.'

The friendly Picc nodded and turned back to look at Trixie, who by now was trying to sit up.

'Oooh! My head,' she said rubbing it gently and looked up at the crowd.

'BOUNCY! Is that you?' shouted Trixie when she saw him. She tried to stand up and then sat down again quickly holding her injured ankle.

'I don't believe it,' she said laughing.

Bouncey rushed to her. 'Don't get up. You're hurt,' he said in a worried voice

'It's not too bad,' replied Trixie.

'Now tell me how you got here. Nobody is supposed to know about this place?'

Bouncey explained how he had gone swimming and of how he had got this far. 'But never mind me. Why are you here and how did you get hurt?'

'I've come to warn the Piccs that the Goblins are getting ready to steal all of their spider's silken thread. They are planning to come tomorrow.' said Pixie.

'I banged my head when I tripped and twisted my ankle at the same time when I escaped from the Goblins this morning. That's after I found out about their plans.'

'How can we stop them?' said Bouncey in a concerned voice.

'If only I could get a message to my friend, the Wizard.'

Trixie sat thinking and then looked at Bouncey and said, 'I have an idea that might work. Do you think the Piccs could get in touch with my friend, Tawnie the Owl and ask her to come here?'

The Piccs have always had a secret way of passing messages between animals and people. They quickly agreed to ask Tawnie the Owl to come as fast as she could fly to their big hut.

They had just finished having something to eat and drink when Tawnie arrived.

Now Trixie the Pixie also had a special power to talk to the animals of the forest but only if they were nearby.

So as soon as Tawnie had rested for a while, Trixie closed her eyes and thought about Tawnie taking a message to the Wizard. To get there and back in time Tawnie would have to fly through the night.

Tawnie nodded her head.

Bouncey had already written a note for the Wizard explaining their problem and could the Wizard help them.

So as soon as the note was tied to one of her legs, Tawnie flew off as quickly as she could.

'Will the Wizard really help us Bouncey?' asked Trixie,

looking quite worried and upset.

'Of course he will,' said Bouncey, as he crossed his fingers behind his back.

The wizard was just getting ready for bed when Tawnie the Owl arrived outside his cave.

'Too Whit! Too Woo! Too Whit! Too Woo!' called Tawnie.

'Good Heavens!' said the wizard. 'It's Tawnie the Owl. What do you want at this time of night?'

Then the Wizard noticed the note tied to her leg. Reading it quickly the Wizard began to tutt and haw, then he tutted and hawed again. 'Yes! That's what I'll do,' he said.

The Wizard knew that the Piccs lived underground, so he went to his magic spell cupboard and took out a small brown bottle.

Looking around his cave the Wizard spied a small hole in the floor. Picking up his long wooden staff he banged the floor with one end of it, three times.

At once a small brown furry face, covered in whiskers, appeared.

It was a tiny mole. Creeping slowly out, it was quickly followed by its best friend.

'Hello, my little beauties,' said the Wizard with a smile. 'I have a little job for both of you. Do you mind?'

Both of the little moles nodded their heads.

'Good,' said the Wizard. 'This is what I want you to do.'

Bending down he put his hands on the top of each mole's head. A noise made the Wizard stop and look up. He saw his big black cat, Ebbo, sitting on the top of his magic spell cupboard, watching carefully.

Bending down again, the Wizard whispered a spell that only the two moles heard.

The magic spell made sure that the moles understood what they had to do once they had seen Bouncey the Elf.

The Wizard then carefully placed the two moles into a small cage. They would be all right because he would send them to sleep all through Tawnie's flight back to the Piccs. He also put the small brown bottle, which contained the magic spell and a note for Bouncey, into the cage as well.

'Now then Tawnie, lets fix you up. Are you ready?' The Wizard asked kindly, as he tied the small cage holding the two sleeping moles, to her leg.

Tawnie was big and strong enough to carry the cage and she nodded her head.

It was still the middle of the night as Tawnie flew back to the Piccs, Bouncey and Trixie. Arriving just before sunrise, well before the Goblins would be ready to raid the Piccs tunnels.

'Well done!' said Trixie when she saw Tawnie and gave her a hug before taking the cage holding the moles off her leg.

Bouncey looked as surprised as Trixie was when he saw the moles in the cage but the note from the Wizard told him what to do. He explained to the Piccs the Wizard's plan.

They had to save the spiders' cavern from the Goblins, making sure that all the silken thread was well hidden.

Everyone helped to block the entrance to the spiders cavern, piling lumps of rock quarried by some of the Piccs in another cave.

Then, making sure they had brought plenty of food and drink, they waited for the Goblins.

Trixie wanted Bouncey to tell her again what was going to happen, She had not been paying attention the first time.

Bouncey just smiled and said.

'Watch and listen.'

Suddenly, they heard the Goblins on the other side of the pile of rocks, which blocked their way. They did not sound very pleased.

As soon as Bouncey heard the Goblins moving some of the rocks, he went to the mole's cage and took them out. 'Okay,' he said. 'Now it's your turn to help us.'

Holding the tiny moles in one hand, Bouncy gave each of them a small drop from the Wizard's magic brown bottle.

There was a big blue flash and the two moles jumped out of Bouncey's hand, onto the floor.

Then they began to grow and grow.

'Wow,' said Trixie and Bouncey together. Even the Piccs were blinking and blinking.

The two moles stopped growing when they reached the size of a small horse.

'That's it,' said Bouncey. 'The Wizard told me this was going to happen, although it still surprised me.'

Turning to his Picc friend, Bouncey asked him to open the tunnel door, which led from the spiders cavern. As soon as the door opened the two, now giant moles, dashed through. They already knew what to do.

As soon as the tunnel door was closed, Bouncey told everyone that they now had to wait.

'What about the Goblins,' cried Trixie, they're still trying to get through the rocky wall we made.

'Don't worry' said Bouncey. 'Just listen.'

So everyone listened, they could hear the Goblins scrabbling on the other side of the rock pile. They heard a shout and then screams. Then silence.

A trickle of water began to flow from under the pile of rocks blocking the entrance to the spiders cavern.

'Look!' cried Trixie, pointing to the where the water was coming into the cavern.

'It's all right.' Bouncey said. 'The moles went to the big pool and made a new tunnel down to where the Goblins were. The clever moles left before the tunnel flooded and washed the horrible Goblins away. They're quite safe and back to their normal size. Most of the Goblins are half way down the River of Dreams by now. In fact, I would say that they are near to their Goblins' Lair, thank goodness.'

The Piccs were over the moon (if they had had one) and insisted that Bouncey take a present of a set of new spiders' silk thread clothes, including shoes.

'Flips!' said Bouncey, 'I had forgotten all about this smelly tunic I borrowed from the Fisher-Piccs.'

'Never mind,' blinked Bouncey's Picc friend, 'nobody else would wear it anyway.'

Everyone laughed or blinked.

Aerie the Faery
and the
White Swan

'I'm bored.'

Aerie the Faery said to Trixie, as she stretched her wings, arms and legs at the same time.

Both the faery and the pixie were sitting by the River of Dreams, enjoying a picnic in the sunshine.

Suddenly, Trixie turned and looked down the river.

'Oh!' she cried out loudly.

'One of my friends, Penn the Swan is hurt.'

Pixies are known to be able to talk to the creatures of the forest and often sense when they need help.

'Where's your friend Penn,' Aerie asked in a worried voice.

'Somewhere near the edge of Fawn Wood, not too far away,' answered the Pixie.

'You know, where that old tree fell across the river.'

Aerie thought for a moment and then said,

'We have some food and drink left from our picnic, so I think we should fly there as soon as we can put everything away in our bags.'

In a very short while, Aerie and Trixie were flying along the banks of the River of Dreams.

They soon reached the old tree lying across the river. Tangled amongst some of the branches of the tree, which trailed in the river, they saw their friend Penn the Swan.

'Look!' cried Aerie. 'Penn is stuck in those branches. Why doesn't she swim free?

Trixie closed her eyes for a moment, then said, 'Penn says one of her wings is broken and she can't move,'

89

After landing by the old fallen tree, Aerie and Trixie walked to the edge of the river.

Penn the swan was wedged between the riverbank and a large branch, which drooped into the river.

Aerie, being the tallest, crawled along the fallen tree trunk, reached out and tried to grab hold of the drooping branch.

'Be careful', shouted Trixie.

Turning to look at Trixie, Aerie slipped off the tree trunk and her feet went into the river.

'Ohhhh! It's cold,' cried Aerie as the river water sloshed into her shoes.

'Are you all right, Aerie?' Trixie called out.

Aerie carefully pulled herself back onto the tree trunk. Her shoes felt squelchy and horrible.

'Yes thanks, Trixie,'

Once more Aerie reached out to the drooping branch, this time she was able to pull it out of the river.

Trixie could then lean over to Penn and gently help her out of the river.

Aerie squelched her way back to help Trixie get Penn safely further up the riverbank.

'Can you ask Penn what happened?'

'Yes I can,' said Trixie as she closed her eyes. A moment or two later, Trixie said. 'Penn and her family and all of her friends have been captured by the Goblins and are being held in cages by Mirror Lake. Her wing got broken when she escaped.'

'Oh! What horrible, cruel creatures,' said Aerie.

'First thing we must do though is help Penn.'

'I know what to do,' said Trixie, as she bent down to Penn and gently straightened the broken wing. It didn't hurt Penn because Trixie used her special gift.

'Now I'll just cover the injured wing with a dab of my secret ointment. That should stop it hurting whilst it gets better,' Trixie told Aerie as she got her special ointment from her shoulder bag.

Aerie and Trixie then had a drink and something to eat from some of their picnic leftovers.

After they had finished their meal, Aerie decided that they had to help Penn rescue her captured family and friends from the horrible goblins.

'How can we do that,' exclaimed Trixie.' There are only two of us.'

'Well,' said Aerie. 'I think I can get more help when we reach Mirror Lake.'

'Are you sure?' Trixie wasn't convinced that Aerie knew of anyone who could beat the Goblins.

'Just for now,' replied Aerie, 'We'd better get a move on before the Goblins hurt anyone else.'

After making sure that Penn was well enough and wanted to travel with them to Mirror Lake, the two friends made their plans.

They decided to go up the River of Dreams because it went near the lake and because it was the only way

Penn could travel. She would be all right in the river but of course she could not fly or even walk far. (Swans can only waddle a short distance on land).

So, Aerie and Trixie walked and now and then flew, (faeries and pixies don't like to fly long distances) to save their aching feet, while Penn bravely paddled up the River of Dreams.

The group of rescuers had been travelling for about three hours, when Aerie heard the sound of a waterfall. It seemed to be round the next river bend.

'Lets stop here for a few minutes,' Aerie said. 'I think we should have a rest.'

'I don't mind having a look,' Trixie said. 'I'm not too tired.'

So, while Aerie and Penn flopped down on the riverbank, Trixie flew round the river bend and saw a lovely sight.

Tumbling down the far side of a rocky pool was a waterfall. Sunlight shining through the falling water made a rainbow and the splashes twinkled like diamonds.

Trixie could see that the path went round the pool to the edge of the waterfall. Then it went through an arch of flowering bushes.

I think we could pass here all right, she thought.

A few minutes later, Aerie and Trixie were coaxing Penn through the pool. The splashing waterfall had frightened her.

Then, suddenly, the pool seemed to explode. A huge shape leapt out of the water and fell back with a tremendous crash.

'A pike! A giant pike,' screamed Aerie.

Penn hissed in alarm, as the pike circled round her.

Then the huge pike dived under Penn and grabbed one of her webbed feet.

Penn hissed in pain as the giant pike tried to pull her underwater into the deep pool.

Trixie, who had stood still, frozen with shock, by the sudden attack of the giant pike, jumped into the pool. She would save her friend.

Swimming as fast as she could, Trixie managed to grab hold of the giant pike as it struggled with Penn.

Holding as tightly as she could to the slippery scales of the giant pike, Trixie closed her eyes and with her special magical gift ordered the giant pike to let go of Penn's foot.

The giant pike was so startled by the sudden thoughts of Trixie, it let go of Penn anyway. Trixie watched with glee as the giant pike raced with a flurry of leaps and splashes, away from the pool.

Penn was safe.

Coughing and spluttering, Trixie staggered to the side of the pool where Aerie was trying to comfort poor Penn.

Fortunately, Trixie had left her shoulder bag by the pool and it was nice and dry.

Inside the bag, the special ointment was really useful again, as Trixie put some on Penn's foot, which had been badly bitten by the giant pike.

When they all had got their breath back, Aerie thanked Trixie for saving Penn.

Penn hissed her agreement.

'What are we to do now?' Trixie asked in a worried voice. 'Penn can't go up the river now with her injured foot.'

Just then a splash in the pool behind them made them all jump but it wasn't the giant pike. It was a giant turtle.

Trixie gave a squeal of delight. 'It's Tam the Turtle.'

Now some say that Tam the giant Turtle swam up the River of Dreams from the Lost Sea, many years ago. In fact, some elves believe that he came up over a hundred and fifty years ago.

Tam the Turtle now lives in his new home under the

main bridge over the River of Dreams, not far from the village of Bouncey the Elf.

Trixie has known Tam for a long time and is one of his best friends.

Tam often gives Trixie rides. She would sit on top of his great big shell while he paddled slowly along the river.

Aerie smiled at Tam and then asked Trixie if she thought he might be able to help them.

'Of course! Tam. Why didn't I think of that,' laughed Trixie. So, closing her eyes Trixie sent a message to Tam asking if he would carry the injured Penn to Mirror Lake.

'Yes, he will be pleased to help,' said Trixie.

As quickly as they could, Aerie and Trixie helped poor Penn onto Tam's giant shell. Fortunately there was just enough room.

Very carefully, Tam slowly carried Penn along the path by the waterfall, eventually reaching the river again.

Tam looked quite tired, he was not used to walking far. So Aerie said that they needed to rest for a while.

After their rest, they set off. Tam much happier now, being back in the river, even though Penn's weight on his back meant that his head was just out of the water and he could only paddle slowly.

Some time later, Aerie and Trixie both started to look worried. The river was now quite near Wild Boar Forest.

The wild boar is very fierce and dangerous. Even Trixie with her special powers took extra care whenever she was in their forest.

So the two friends kept a watchful eye, just in case they saw any wild boars. Fortunately, they didn't see any.

Moving, slowly but surely, they went further and farther upriver until Aerie said, in a loud voice.

'Stop! Stop right now!'

'Why? What's the matter?' asked Trixie, looking a bit scared.

'We're not far from the Goblins' Lair.' answered Aerie.

'Oooohhh! What can we do?' cried Trixie, who, like most of the people of Elfinland, was frightened of the Goblins.

'Let me think for a minute,' said Aerie. 'I might have an

idea that could work. Come over here Trixie and listen to this'. Aerie waved an arm to Trixie.

Tam was really glad for the rest and took the opportunity to nibble a few wild flowers growing next to the river.

So, going over to Aerie, Trixie listened in amazement to Aerie's plan.

'I could do it but I have never done anything like it before,' said Trixie. So, asking Tam and Penn to stay very quiet, Trixie closed her eyes.

Nothing seemed to happen at first. Then a loud whirring and flapping noise could be heard in the forest behind them.

A dark cloud suddenly appeared in the sky above the river. It was no cloud. Birds, thousands and thousands of birds of all kinds darted and swooped around them, then, as if on a signal, they all flew off over the forest.

They were on the way to the Goblins' Lair. Diving, swooping and squawking they made all of the terrified Goblins rush inside their houses and bolt and close all of their doors and windows.

'Now!' cried Aerie, 'we must go as fast as we can and get away from the Goblins.'

Tam was terrific. Even with Penn sitting on his shell he paddled and paddled and paddled his way to safety, whilst Aerie and Trixie flew over them as guides.

After a good rest and something to eat and drink (Tam always had a ready supply of food by the river). Aerie said that they were quite near Mirror Lake.

Going up the smaller side river, which led from the River of Dreams to the edge of Mirror Lake, Aerie, Trixie and Tam with Penn on his shell, quietly reached the shore of the lake.

Hiding behind a large clump of reeds, they could see a horrible sight. A long row of cages, were next to the lake. Crowded inside of them were the family and friends of Penn.

Not far away from the cages was the Goblin camp, a line of tents full of the horrible Goblins.

'Why do the Goblins need the swans?' asked Aerie, 'And keep them in cages.'

'Just a minute' said Trixie. 'I'm trying to find out.' She closed her eyes and concentrated very hard. The captured swans told Trixie that the Goblins had discovered that there were hundreds of pearls at the bottom of Mirror Lake.

Pearls can sometimes be found in fresh water mussels (a shellfish). The special magical water of Mirror Lake has made these pearls extra large and more valuable.

'The Goblins are using the captured swans to bring up the mussels from the bottom of the lake,' Trixie told Aerie.

'That's terrible,' said Aerie. 'We must rescue all of Penn's family and friends as soon as we can.'

'How can we do that?' said Trixie. 'There are so many Goblins.'

'I have a special friend who lives near here,' said Aerie with a smile. 'Just watch.'

Holding her arms wide, Aerie lifted up her head and said in a loud voice,

'Athan, Keeper of the Unicorns, it is I, Aerie. I come to claim my reward for saving a young Unicorn. Please help he swans and drive away the Goblins.'

Suddenly, the surface of Mirror Lake misted over. Then the mist became a thick cloud.

A quiet voice spoke from inside of it. 'Hello Aerie, this is Athan speaking. We know that your friends are in need of help. Because of my promise, you shall receive it.'

'Now,' said Athan. 'Do not move from where you are. No matter what you see happening. Do you understand Aerie.'

'Yes,' replied Aerie, wondering what was about to happen.

The cloud began to get bigger and bigger. A sound of hooves grew like thunder and out of the cloud a herd of white unicorns came racing straight towards the Goblins' camp.

Within seconds the Goblin camp was in ruins and all the Goblins had run away, most of them into the Barren Mountains, never to be seen again.

Turning round Aerie saw that the cloud was turning to a mist again and the unicorns were nearly out of sight. Quickly, before it was gone she shouted.

'Athan, Athan,' she called.

'Thank you thank you and all of your unicorn friends. We will never forget your help. Bye.'

Aerie then turned to Trixie. 'Come on Trixie. We have a lot to do.'

It took ages to get all of Penn's family and friends out of the cages. They were all so happy to be free again.

'What should we do now,' Aerie asked Trixie after a rest and something to eat.

'Well!' said Trixie, 'I'm going to stay with Penn and her family and friends until they are all feeling well enough to travel. What about you?'

Aerie thought for a moment and said, 'I'm going to hitch a ride with Tam and take it easy for a while.'

Tam nodded in agreement.

Then Penn gave a loud hiss.

'That was a big thank you from Penn,' said Trixie.

'Oh! By the way Aerie, the next time you want me to come to one of your riverside picnics. I might say no,' Trixie the Pixie said with a big smile.

Skipper the Kangaroo
has a
Desert Adventure

It was hot in the desert. So hot that the two young kangaroos, Skipper and his best friend Legs, were looking for a shady place to rest in. They were lost and trying to find their way home.

The heat of the sun was making them feel dizzy as they slowly climbed up a small hill.

As they passed a jumble of rocks Skipper saw a dark hole, partly hidden by one big boulder.' Legs! Legs!' he shouted. 'Look a cave.'

Legs slowly lifted his head and looked at the cave. 'Will it be cooler inside?' he asked hopefully.

'Yes, it will be,' said Skipper. 'Come on hurry. Let's get inside away from this heat as fast as we can.'

'Oooh! That's nice,' said Legs a short time later. He was lying down, deep inside the cool shade of the cave. He then closed his eyes and dozed off.

A loud noise woke Skipper. 'What was that?' He rubbed his eyes and mumbled to himself. 'I must have fallen asleep.'

He was moving around Legs, who was still asleep on the cave floor, when a sudden clap of thunder made him jump. Looking out of the cave, Skipper saw rain pouring down the hillside, into a fast flowing river.

He also noticed that it was now much cooler than it was before.

Skipper shivered and moved further back into the darkness of the large cave.

A flash of lightning lit the cave and showed his friend Legs curled up, his eyes big and wide open, looking very scared.

'Don't worry, Legs,' Skipper said to his younger best friend. 'It's only a thunderstorm.'

'I know,' said Legs.

'But I still don't like the sound of thunder. It gives me earache.'

'Pitter, Patter. Patter, Pitter.' The rain outside the cave seemed to be talking.

'Splish! Splash! Splosh! Splish! Splash! Splosh! Have a wash!'

'How long do we have to stay here?' asked Legs. I'm getting hungry.'

'Not long, I hope,' said Skipper.

'In fact I think the rain is stopping now.'

Sure enough, the dark thunderclouds were now getting much brighter and a sunbeam shone straight into their cave.

'Oooh, that's better,' said Legs, getting up onto his extra long hind legs (hence his name) and stretching his two much smaller front paws. 'Lets go and get something to eat.'

'Good idea,' said Skipper leading the way from the cave, down towards the river.

There was plenty of grass down by the flooded river, which was flowing very fast and deep because of all the rain.

Skipper and Legs began to eat the grass as quickly as they could.

Munch, Munch, Munch, Munch. They were really hungry.

Afterwards, hopping down to the river for a drink of water, Legs suddenly shouted. 'Look over there, Skipper.'

A large tree was stuck, with one of its branches making a sort of bridge to the riverbank.

'I bet you can't climb onto that tree?' Legs dared.

'Well,' said Skipper looking carefully at the big tree, which was bobbing up and down in the flooded river.

'I.... I....'

'You're scared aren't you', laughed Legs as he walked along the branch, which was sticking out from the tree.

'No I'm not!' shouted Skipper.

'And be careful, that branch is all wet and slippery.'

'Come on, it's dead easy!' Legs went further along the slippery branch by clinging to some of the smaller side ones.

Taking a deep breath, Skipper began to follow him. Carefully and slowly he made his way behind Legs, who by now, was on the main trunk of the tree.

'Hurry up slow coach!' Legs called, 'It's great being out here!'

Skipper reached the spot where Legs had stopped. 'I don't think this is a good idea,' he said as the big tree rocked too and fro.

'This is super. I like this!' Legs cried and he began to jump up and down making the bobbing worse.

'Stop jumping,' shouted Skipper but Legs was enjoying himself far too much to stop.

'Oh no,' Skipper cried, as the big tree bobbed and rocked so much. It was suddenly swept away by the rushing water of the river.

The two friends were now adrift on a big tree in the middle of the river.

'What do we do now?' cried Legs in alarm, as he held on tightly to the nearest tree branch.

The racing flood had taken the big tree to the centre of the river and had then begun to swirl it around and around.

'I feel dizzy,' complained Legs.

'Can we get off now?'

'Don't be silly,' said Skipper calmly.

'How do you think we can reach the riverbank? It's miles away.'

It wasn't really but the river must have been quite deep to float the big tree and it was moving so fast, it would have been very dangerous to even try it.

Skipper looked round and found a safe place to sit down. 'Come and sit by me, Legs.'

'All right! I'm coming.'

Taking great care, Legs moved to where Skipper was sitting.

The two friends watched the riverbanks flash by as they raced down river, now and then swirling around and around in a big circle.

They must have travelled for miles and miles before Skipper said.

'Do you see them?'

'What can you see?' asked Legs, looking around. All he could see were rows and rows of trees lining the river. 'I can't see anything.'

'There!' Skipper pointed with one paw.

A large flock of cockatoos were flying in and out of a clump of trees, not too far ahead.

As the big tree floated closer to the cockatoos, Skipper gave a loud shout.

The flock of birds started to squawk among themselves and then began to fly off in all directions.

Suddenly, one of the cockatoos turned round and flew back toward Skipper and Legs.

'Why are you two floating in the middle of the river?' the big white bird asked. 'I thought Kangaroos lived on the ground.'

'We do, normally,' replied Skipper.

'We sort of got on this tree by accident.'

'Well, what are you going to do now?' said the Cockatoo, curious to know how the strangers were going to get off the floating tree..

'We hoped you could help us,' Skipper told the bird.

'Me! What can I do.'

The Cockatoo then flew down and perched on a branch next to Skipper and Legs.

Skipper had to think hard. How could the bird help them? The first thing though was to be introduced to it.

'Pleased to meet you Skipper and Legs, my name is Cockie,' said the Cockatoo.'

'Well, now we know each other, maybe you could help us Cockie,' Skipper said hopefully.

'We don't know where we are.'

'Oh! I see,' said Cockie.

He closed one eye and cocked his head to one side and then said. 'Well this river, when it is in flood like now, goes into a big lake about ten miles away.'

'Ten miles,' squeaked Legs.

'We'll starve to death before we reach it. We can't get off this floating tree to get something to eat.'

'I know,' said Skipper, 'But what can we do?'

'I've got an idea,' said Cockie excitedly. 'Leave it to me.' And with that he suddenly flew off towards the trees by the riverbank.

A short time later, Skipper and Legs were amazed to see a large flock of cockatoos flying towards them, with Cockie in front. Each of the birds carried a tuft of grass in its claws.

'We won't starve now,' cried Legs as he grabbed a pawful of grass from the nearest cockatoo, and gratefully began to eat.

A while later, Skipper asked Cockie to thank all of his friends for feeding them so well.

'No problem,' said Cockie, who then flew back to join them.

The big tree continued floating down the river towards the lake.

'What are we going to do when we reach the lake, Skipper?' asked Legs.

'I'm not sure,' answered Skipper, trying not to show how worried he really was.

It took about five hours for the river current to carry them all the way down to the lake.

Skipper could hardly see the far shore, the lake was so big and there were waves. Not too large but big enough to make the big tree rock and bob about.

'Oooh!' cried Legs, 'I don't like this. Will we fall into the lake Skipper?'

'I hope not,' replied Skipper.

The big tree seemed to be moving towards a small group of rocks sticking out of the water, from which a few bushes could be seen growing between them.

'Skipper, will we be able to land there. I'm getting very tired of holding onto this tree,' said Legs, looking very miserable.

Before Skipper could answer, the big tree suddenly stopped moving.

'Quickly Legs,' shouted Skipper. 'Jump into the water, now, before the tree starts to move again.'

Swiftly, the two friends jumped into the water and found that they could wade through it and sit on one of the rocks.

'Whew!' said Legs, 'That's better,' as he gave his long legs a good stretch.

Skipper wasn't too sure. Looking around he saw that there were only six or seven large rocks with a few straggly bushes poking up through them.

'We can't stay here for long,' he told Legs. 'There's no food for us to eat.'

'Leave here,' said Legs in an alarmed voice.

'We can't swim to the shore. It's too far.'

'I know,' said Skipper in a worried voice.

The two friends were sitting quietly when a sudden splashing noise made them both look round.

To their amazement, a long dark shape appeared out of the water.

'Hello. I'm Snappie.' A huge mouth full of large sharp teeth smiled at them.

'Haven't you seen a crocodile before?' Snappie asked, as he waddled out of the lake.'

'I... I... think so,' stuttered Skipper, 'But not so near as you are.'

Legs came out from one of the rocks he had scuttled behind, feeling a little silly.

'I certainly haven't. How do you do Snappie.' he said trying to look brave. 'I'm Legs and this is my best friend Skipper.'

'Pleased to meet you,' said Snappie with another big toothy smile.

'Now tell why you are in the middle of Lake Not.'

So Skipper explained how they happened to be in the middle of the lake. 'But, Snappie,' he asked. 'Why did you call this Lake Not?'

'Well now,' said Snappie as he settled down in front of them.

'I have lived around here for over one hundred years.'

'ONE HUNDRED YEARS,' cried Legs in an astonished voice.

'Can anything live that long?'

106

'We do,' smiled Snappie. 'All crocodiles live a very long time. I thought everyone knew that.'

'Anyway, this lake', continued Snappie, 'Is just like most lakes in the desert. They do not last very long because the heat of the sun makes the water dry up.'

'I can't see that happening here,' said Legs with a laugh. Look at all the water in the lake and the river is filling it up all the time.'

'Ah,' said Snappie with a knowing smile.

'Did you know that the river will dry up as well, in a day or two. It was the thunderstorm that provided the rain that flooded the river. The storm has gone. No more rain round here for maybe five or six years. So Legs, the river will dry up and soon so will the lake. That is why we call it Lake Not.'

'How does that help us?' Skipper said. 'We need to get to the shore of the lake but it's too far for us to swim.'

'Ah hem! Listen to me,' explained Snappie. 'If you would like a ride on my back, I could take you both to the lake shore.'

'Yes please,' cried Skipper and Legs together.

'That would be great. Thank you Snappie.'

'Okay. Get on my back and then off we go.'

Snappie gave big toothy grin and turned round carefully.

After climbing onto his back, Skipper and Legs held on tightly as Snappie began to swim slowly towards the shore. It took them about half an hour to get there.

'Wow! That was fun,' said Legs to Skipper.

'Yes, it was,' agreed Skipper, sorry that they had to say goodbye to their new friend.

They waved goodbye as Snappie swam back to the deeper waters of the lake.

'Will we see him again?' Legs asked

'I hope so,' replied Skipper.

'He was a good friend.'

There was plenty of grass around for them to have a good feed and after a short rest they decided to look for a way home.

Hopping at a steady pace they were soon quite a long way from Lake Not.

Skipper thought they should go towards the high ground first, hoping he might remember the right way home.

They were passing through the part of the desert, which had been in the storm. Green plants and flowers of all different colours could be seen everywhere.

It was beautiful, though it wouldn't last for long. The hot desert sun would soon dry out the land and only the cactus plants, hardy grasses and the special kind of trees which needed little water, would survive.

For now though, Skipper and Legs were happy. There was plenty of food and water to drink and they were able to find shady places quite easily.

Then Legs called to Skipper

'I think we are being followed.'

Skipper stopped and looked around.

'I can't see anything Legs. Are you sure you saw something?'

Legs pulled a face. 'I did, honest.'

Then he pointed to a large prickly bush.

'Look! Can you see? It's a big dog.'

'Oh dear!' said Skipper in a worried voice.

'It's not a big dog. That's a Dingo and we are in a lot of trouble.'

He explained to Legs that a grown Dingo hunts kangaroos, especially the young ones, as well as other animals.'

'We need a place to hide in, a place which might stop it getting to us.'

'Can we find a place in time,' Legs wanted to know. 'Before it tries to catch one of us.'

Skipper looked around hopefully but only saw a few bushes.

Then he heard a strange rustling sound coming from near his hind legs. A strange looking creature, quite small, walked into view.

It was about the size of a rabbit and its body was covered in sharp pointed spines.

'Hi! I'm Spikie! I couldn't help over hearing. I think I could help but I'm afraid I can only help one of you. I'm an anteater and I have a den near these bushes. I'm sure one of you might just fit into it, if you keep away from my cubs.'

Before Skipper or Legs could say anything, the Dingo began to howl.

'That's done it,' said Skipper

'Other Dingoes might hear that and come here too.'

'We have no time to lose,' said Legs. 'Skipper, you go with Spikie and I will make the Dingo chase me. It's our only chance,' pleaded Legs.

'Don't forget, I'm not called Legs for nothing.'

Skipper knew it made sense, Legs was the fastest kangaroo he had ever known.

So he agreed to go with Spikie to her den.

'Don't worry about Skipper.' Spikie told Legs.

'I will roll up into a ball and block the entrance with my sharp spines. The Dingo will get a sore nose if he comes near me.'

Skipper and Spikie were soon inside the den. The baby anteaters were all asleep and fortunately for Skipper, their little spines were not sharp.

Legs waited until they were safe and then peeped out from his hiding place behind a small bush, to see if he could see the Dingo.

There, it was still hiding behind the prickly bush.

Slowly Legs crept out of his hiding place and began to hop as though he had hurt a leg.

The Dingo sprang out from behind the prickly bush and rushed towards Legs, its big jaws wide open ready to bite.

Legs gave a great leap that took him over some smaller bushes and raced away into the open desert, the Dingo following as fast as it could run.

The chase lasted a long time.

Up rocky slopes, down through the drying riverbeds and across the flowering ground. Legs ran like the wind.

The Dingo began to slow down. It stopped running and began to stagger and then it fell down, panting.

It could go no further.

Legs had won.

The Dingo would not be able to hunt for a long time to come.

It took Legs ages to return to Skipper and Spikie. He was tired but the welcome he got from his two friends made him feel so much better.

After a good nights sleep, Skipper and Legs said goodbye to their new friend Spikie.

'Come back any time. You are always welcome,' Spikie said as she wished them a safe journey.

Taking a chance, the two friends decided to keep going in the same direction, hoping to see a place they might recognize.

They had been travelling for most of the day in the hot desert sunshine, when Skipper spotted some animals in the distance.

111

They looked quite big, even though they were a long way off.

'I know what they are,' said Legs.

'Camels. I wonder if they are the ones I met a year ago.'

There were five camels in the group. Four were adults and the fifth one appeared half grown.

As Skipper and Legs got near to them, the young camel came rushing up.

'Legs! Is that really you?'

'Humpy,' cried Legs.

'What a surprise to see you here'.

'We have been following the rains,' said Humpy. 'The food is really plentiful around here. What about you two?'

So Skipper and Legs went with Humpy and met his family. They took turns in telling them all about their adventures and how they were trying to find their way back home.

'Can you think of anything about where you came from? We might be able to help,' said Humpy's Dad.

'Well!' Skipper thought for a minute.

'Our families live most of the time in a valley with good grass and the water comes from an underground spring. So most years we don't have to worry about the desert sun drying everything up,' he said.

'Oh! And there is a big mountain which has three funny shaped lumps near the top.'

'We know of that place,' said Humpy's dad. 'Tomorrow Humpy will take you there. We will follow you in a few days and see you all there. OK!'

'You bet,' cried Legs and Skipper together and they went with Humpy to make plans for their journey.

Early the next day, the three friends set off. As usual it was bright and sunny and they made a good start.

By the middle of the afternoon they decided to stop next to a watering hole, which was nicely shaded by a big tree.

Feeling tired after the long trip, they all lay down and began to doze.

'Hey! Wake up,' a strange voice called to them.

'I wouldn't sleep there if I were you.'

Skipper opened one eye and looked around. Sitting by the watering hole, a giant frog was looking at him.

'Why wouldn't you sleep here?' asked Skipper.'

'Because of that,' said the frog, pointing to a large green and black snake, which was slowly sliding down the tree trunk.

'Wake up. Quick,' shouted Skipper in a panicky voice

Humpy and Legs jumped up in alarm and seeing the big snake rushed to the other side of the watering hole. Skipper was not far behind them.

'Ha! Ha! That scared you, didn't it,' said the frog, laughing so much he slipped down into the watering hole with a big splash.

'Ugh!' The frog gave a cough and jump back out of the water.

'Sorry about that,' he said in that strange voice of his.

'I couldn't resist it.' I'm Croakie by the way and coming down to meet us is Issie. Don't worry. She won't hurt a fly. That's my job.'

Croakie opened his mouth and a long sticky tongue shot out and caught one, which happened to be sitting on a lily pad.

Issie slid down the rest of the tree trunk and slithered towards them,

'It'sssss sssssso nicccccce to meet you,' she hissed.

Humpy stepped back a pace, bumping into Skipper and Legs, nearly knocking them over.

'Er... Er...' Skipper couldn't get a word out.

So Legs said, 'Hi! Issie. How are things with you? I bet you haven't put a foot wrong today.'

Croakie nearly fell into the watering hole again.

'Did you hear that Issie. Have you put a foot wrong today.' 'Ha! Ha! Ha! That was Brilliant, Legs. Brilliant.'

Skipper saw that his two friends did not like the way Issie was staring at them.

She had stopped a few metres away and her head was swaying in a funny way.

This Way. That Way. This Way. That Way. This Way. That Way.

Her large eyes were black and shiny and a long thin forked tongue, flicked in and out between the two long fangs of her wide-open mouth. It was making him feel quite dizzy.

Shaking his head so that he could think more clearly, Skipper told a fib to Croakie and Issie.

'Oh! I've just remembered.

'We shall have to be going now. A friend of ours is waiting at the next watering-hole.'

'What a shame,' said Croakie, with a wink of a large eye.

'I know Issie wanted to squeeze you in for dinner tonight.'

'Ha. Ha. Ha,' he laughed loudly.

'Squeeze you in for dinner. Do you get it?'

He laughed again, 'Ha. Ha. Ha.'

But the three friends had already left the watering hole, Legs saying how glad he was not to be staying for dinner with Croakie and Issie

After spending the night huddled together between two large boulders, making sure that there were no big lizards about, they ate some grass and then went on, following a faint track, which led to the mountains.

Humpy said they were going the right way because he had been on this track before.

Legs spotted the strange mountain shape first, shouting out to his friends excitedly.

'Look. We're here.'

'Yes, that's it,' said Skipper.

'That's the Mountain with Three Lumps. We're nearly home.'

It was nearly dark when they arrived at the valley where all the kangaroo families lived

What a big surprise they got when Skipper, Legs and Humpy called out to them.

The families of Skipper and Legs were so happy to see them back safe and unharmed.

Then they thanked Humpy for his help.

By now, Humpy was surrounded by lots of young kangaroos, who had never seen a camel before, asking him all sorts of questions;

'Humpy why are all your legs the same size?'

'Humpy, Humpy, is that lump on your back heavy?'

'Humpy, why are your feet so big?'

Smiling happily, Humpy began to answer all their eager questions.

Bouncey the Elf
and the Goblin Goldmine

One day, Bouncey the Elf, decided to go for a walk in the forest. Packing his backpack with a bottle of pop and some of his favourite biscuits, he was soon ready to go on his trip.

Bouncey set off by crossing the bridge over the River of Dreams. He had only been in the forest for a few minutes, when he heard the sound of something moving through the bushes.

He stood still and watched. A baby deer came into view. The fawn stopped and with big, round startled eyes, looked around. Then it ran off down a little path not far from where Bouncy stood.

After waiting for a few minutes, Bouncey decided to follow the baby deer. He trotted down the path for some time - first turning to the right - then to the left, until he came to a small stream.

As Bouncy watched, the little fawn had a drink, then it jumped over the small stream and went to what he thought was a big bush.

'Oh look', Bouncy thought to himself, realizing it wasn't a bush. What he thought were branches were actually the giant antlers of a daddy deer.

The animals were both very pleased to see each other and rubbed noses. Then, without a sound, they disappeared into the forest.

Bouncey looked around and realized he had no idea where he was. He was lost.

So he began to look for the right path.

Suddenly, he heard a noise – a strange, funny sound. Feeling afraid, Bouncey knew right away what it was.

'Oh no, not Goblins!' he said to himself in alarm.

Hiding behind a small bush, he saw two strangely dressed Goblins go by.

They wore funny looking hats, with candles fixed to them and they each carried a sack and a hammer.

The Goblins then went behind a big tree.

So, Bouncey being Bouncey, crept after them and saw a large cave behind the tree.

Suddenly, there was a flash of light - the two Goblins were lighting the candles on each of their helmets.

He watched carefully as they disappeared into the cave

When the candlelight was very faint, Bouncey crept to the cave entrance. There were little stone steps cut into the floor.

Very quietly Bouncey set off, down a long dark tunnel carved into the rock.

Crash! Thud! Crash! The sound of banging echoed all through the tunnel.

Bouncey looked through the gloom of the tunnel and could see a light in the distance. He could just see the shadowy forms of the Goblins. They had lit another candle and had stuck it on a big rock by the tunnel wall.

He crept nearer, they were banging the wall of the tunnel with their hammers and big lumps of rock fell to the floor of the cave. The rock was shiny and it glittered and gleamed in the candlelight, a bright yellow colour. Bouncey could hardly believe his eyes.

It must be gold, he thought gleefully.

As he watched, the Goblins knocked more of the shining yellow rock onto the floor of the cave.

When they had a big pile, they stopped and filled their two sacks. Then, turning round, they started back the way they had come.

Fortunately, just in time, Bouncey quickly found a little hollow in the wall of the tunnel, to squeeze into.

He held his breath, as the Goblins staggered by him, with their heavy loads, muttering to each other all the time, their low voices slowly fading in the distance.

He was very glad to see them go. Goblins are really greedy, mean and nasty creatures. They can smell the best gold deep underground and they always wanted to keep it for themselves.

Now Bouncey knew that the Elf King would like some of the glistening golden rocks.

So when all seemed clear, Bouncey went over to the pile of gold rock, which he could only just see in the gloom of the now small candle flickering on the large rock.

He put two big rocks of gold into his backpack and quietly and slowly made his way back to the entrance of the cave and climbed out.

Carefully, looking and listening for any sign of the Goblins, Bouncey made quite sure that they had gone.

Spotting a little track he hadn't seen before, he followed it through the forest until he came to the path that the little baby deer had used earlier that day.

Before long he had reached the stream and then the place where he had first seen the little fawn.

'Goody! I know where I am now,' he said to himself.

Bouncy happily skipped and bounced his way back to the Elf Village, even if he had a much heavier backpack.

When he arrived at the Elf Village gates, the guards told him to go straight to the Elf Kings' Palace.

So Bouncey went into the Palace and found the Elf King waiting for him.

'Hello, Bouncey' said the Elf King cheerfully. 'What have you been up to today?'

Bouncey smiled but didn't say a word. Still smiling he took off his backpack and turned it upside down in front of the Elf King.

Out fell his bottle of pop and a packet of biscuits.

The Elf King started to laugh - but then... the two large gleaming gold rocks dropped onto the floor - with a loud thud!

The Elf King was astonished and very, pleased.

He knew that Goblin gold is much more precious than any other gold - it is so much brighter

'We can make some wonderful things with this.' said the Elf King with a big smile.

'Necklaces, rings and maybe some golden plates. Well done, Bouncey, well done.'

The Elf King then asked Bouncey to tell him all over again, his exciting adventure with the Goblins.

As a reward, the Elf King allowed Bouncey to go down to the royal kitchens, to choose whatever he fancied.

He was soon enjoying a meal of a chocolate milk–shake, a honey and peanut-butter sandwich and then, a huge strawberry ice - cream cornet, covered with chocolate syrup.

A few days later, the Elf King sent him a present of a very special golden goblet, which had been made from the Goblin gold.

Whenever Bouncey drank from it, he thought of his adventure in the forest, which had led him to the Goblin's gold.

For some reason though, he never could find that Goblin goldmine again. Perhaps he needed the little fawn to show him the way.

Eddy the Lifeboat
and the
Seal Island Rescue

Eddy the Lifeboat slid down the ramp of the lifeboat station, and crashed into the sea with a great big - sssplash!

'There's been a call for help,' explained the Captain to Eddy.

'A small plane has crashed on the cliffs above Sandy Bay, Seal Island. We have to try and rescue the crew.'

'Okay - let's get going, as fast as we can then,' answered Eddy. He put on full-speed ahead as they raced towards Seal Island.

They had been going about half an hour when the Captain shouted.

'I say! Eddy! There's something wrong with your compass. The needle's spinning round and round.'

The compass was very important. It told Eddy which way to go.

'That is a big problem,' Eddy said in a worried voice.

After another five minutes the Captain ordered Eddy to stop the engine.

'We'll be going round and round in circles if we keep going on like this' said the Captain.

'Not only that, if we're not careful, we'll have to send out for a rescue party for ourselves.'

While they were bobbing up and down on the waves wondering what to do, a shrill voice suddenly piped up.

'Hello Eddy!'

Eddy looked down and what a surprise he got, there was Sal the Seal in the water.

'Why have you stopped?' enquired Sal curiously. 'You're usually dashing round trying to save people.'

Eddy explained what had happened. Seal Island was a long way and without the compass they were lost.

Sal the Seal was a very clever and helpful seal. She had an idea.

'If I swim in front of you, can you follow me?' asked Sal.

'I'm sure I can,' replied Eddy.

With the help of the Captain and a sailor who was on deck to make sure they didn't go too near, Eddy the Lifeboat chugged steadily on, following Sal the Seal as she swam slowly ahead.

They were not travelling at their usual hectic speed but at least they were going the right way.

About an hour later they saw the mountains of Seal Island and the high cliffs that plunged into the sea.

'Nearly there!' shouted Eddy above the sound of the engine and the splashing waves.

'Yes, I can smell the seaweed on the rocks,' Sal the Seal shouted back.

'I can hear my friends too. I think I'll join them now.'

'Fine,' said Eddy, 'And thank you Sal, we'll be all right now.'

'Any time,' answered Sal the Seal.

'Just give me a shout if you need me on the way back.'

Sal the Seal then swam to join her friends basking in the sunshine on the rocks at the foot of the cliffs.

Eddy slowly circled around the rocks, which could be so dangerous. Many ships had been wrecked there, so he his way slowly to the far side of the island where the plane had come down.

When he got there, Eddy saw a small beach with a high cliff rising steeply above it. At the top of the cliff they could see the crashed plane. Next to it, two figures were waving frantically.

'Now,' said the Captain.

'Let's see how near the shore we can get.'

So Eddy went as close to the beach as he dared. The sea was shallow enough for two sailors to jump down with a big rope and wade out to the shore. They then tied the rope tightly to a huge rock, so that Eddy would not float away.

One sailor, who was also an experienced climber, took hold of a much thinner rope and started to climb up the cliff, which fortunately was not as difficult to climb as it looked.

When he got to the top, he shouted down that the two airmen weren't badly injured and would be able to get down with some help.

So the sailor fastened spare ropes to both men in turn and soon they were lowered to the bottom of the cliff.

He then clambered down himself, knocking some loose pebbles down, which bounced onto the beach below with a loud clatter amongst the rocks, just missing the other waiting men.

The three quickly crossed the little beach and waded through the sea and arrived safe and sound on the deck of Eddy the Lifeboat.

The two pale and shaken airmen were taken below deck, given clean dry clothes and hot chocolate to drink.

'Well done,' said the Captain to the sailor who had rescued the two airmen.

The big rope was then untied from the rock and when the sailor was back onboard, Eddy was able to slowly back away from the beach.

'Well,' said the Captain, 'I think we'll need Sal the Seal to help us again. The compass is still not working properly.'

He sounded Eddy's hooter - twice.

Blaaaahhh! Blaaaahhh!

Hearing the hooter, Sal the Seal soon was splashing alongside Eddy the Lifeboat.

'Can you guide us again Sal,' asked Eddy. 'We've got to get back to the Lifeboat Station and my compass is still broken.'

'Certainly,' said Sal the Seal with a playful look in her eyes.

'Just don't go too fast and run me over, will you?'

'Okay Sal, I'll be careful,' replied Eddy with a big smile.

'Carefully now! Slow ahead Eddy,' ordered the Captain.

Sal knew exactly which way to go and she led Eddy and his crew slowly and steadily across the sea towards the Lifeboat Station.

It took a long time.

Although Sal the Seal was a good swimmer, she rarely swam such long distances and she had to keep stopping for a rest. Every time she stopped, the cook threw defrosted pieces of fish into the water for Sal to eat.

After several long hours, they arrived back at the Lifeboat Station.

Everyone at the Lifeboat Station cheered Sal the Seal, after they had heard the part she had played, in the rescue.

The two airmen from the plane were whisked away to hospital for a check up.

Sal the Seal stayed in the water and rested for some time, very pleased to be the centre of attraction.

Eventually she dived under the sea and turned for home.

'Well done Eddy,' congratulated the Captain. 'I'm glad you've got friends like Sal the Seal.'

'I'm glad too,' replied Eddy. 'It would have looked a bit silly having another Lifeboat rescue me!'

Bouncey the Elf
and the
River of Dreams

Sunlight was shining brightly through the branches of the giant Sleep Tree, which was shading Bouncey the Elf nicely from the hot sunshine. He was lying comfortably in the long grass by the giant tree.

The Sleep Tree grew by the River of Dreams, which flowed through Wild Boar Forest. Bouncey often came here to meet his many friends. Not in person but in the world of his dreams.

Anyone who fell asleep by the Sleep Tree was spirited away into another world where you could talk and play with your friends or just enjoy what they are doing.

The Sleep Tree allowed a person to go on a sleep journey only once a month.

So if you wanted to meet a sleep friend, a visit was a must. It was the only place where the magic would work.

Today, Bouncey wanted to see if his friend Trixie the Pixie, would like to talk to him. So, lying comfortably in the tall grass next to the giant Sleep Tree, Bouncey dozed off and was soon fast asleep.

A shadow fell across Bouncey's face and he woke up. 'Who's that?' he asked looking around.

'Hi Bouncey, it's me,' said Trixie with a big smile.

Then, before Bouncey could say anything, Trixie spoke on in a worried voice.

'Oh! Bouncey, Elfinland is in terrible trouble. The River of Dreams is beginning to dry up.'

'What!' cried Bouncey in an alarmed voice.

'How can the River of Dreams dry up? It's the biggest river in Elfinland. Anyway Trixie. How do you know so much about it?'

'Well,' said Trixie.

You know my friend Tawnie the Owl, don't you? She sent me a thought message that she had seen some Trolls blocking the river which comes out of Mirror Lake.'

(Pixies have a special magical power to 'speak' through thinking, with all the wild animals of the land).

'No more water is coming down from Mirror Lake into the River of Dreams.'

'Wow,' said Bouncey.

'That is bad news.'

'That's not all,' Trixie went on. 'The main River of Dreams starts in the Barren Mountains and that too, says Tawnie, is drying up as well. The Trolls must have gone on to there too.'

'What can I do to help,' Bouncey asked Trixie. 'Elfinland needs the River of Dreams to water farm crops and things.'

'Well,' said Trixie.' I think we should go and see the Wizard and ask if he could give us some ideas and maybe some magic things to help us stop these horrible Trolls from doing any more harm to Elfinland.'

'Okay, let's meet at the Wizard's cave as soon as we can,' Bouncey said.

'Good idea,' Trixie replied. Then she disappeared.

'Ooops,' said Bouncey, looking up through the branches of the Sleep Tree. 'I had forgotten I was in a dream sleep.'

Scrambling up to his feet, Bouncey rushed home to put a few things for a journey into his backpack.

In five ticks he was on his way to the Wizard's cave. Crossing the bridge over a now shallower River of Dreams, Bouncey raced through Fawn Wood.

Then making sure that he kept clear of Wild Boar Forest, he began to climb a steep path, which would lead him through the hills towards the Wizard's cave.

Tired and very thirsty, Bouncey at last reached the Wizard's cave where he saw that Trixie the Pixie was already there.

His dream had actually come true.

'I wish I had wings like you Trixie,' he said when he reached her. I'm worn out with all this rushing.'

'Yes, they are useful,' she said.

'But don't forget I can only fly for short distances. I used them today to get over the steep parts of the path. That's why I got here first.'

'Now then! Now then! What have we here,' the Wizard said as he suddenly appeared from nowhere.

'How nice to see you both,' he said, smiling at them. Then with a click of his fingers, two glasses of fruit smoothies jumped into his hands.

'Have a drink to cool you down while you tell me why you have come all this way to see me,' the Wizard said kindly.

The Wizard began to stroke his long beard when Bouncey had finished telling him their story.

'My goodness me! My goodness me!' the Wizard said as he began to walk around his cauldron which was smoking and bubbling in the middle of his cave.

'How can I help?' he asked them.

'Well,' said Bouncey and Trixie together.

'Hold on, hold on,' laughed the Wizard.

'One at a time.'

'We need to get to Mirror Lake first,' said Trixie.'

'And we need to get there quickly as well,' Bouncey added.

'Also, do you think you could give us some of that magic potion I once borrowed from you a long time ago --- Please?'

The Wizard smiled as he remembered the first time he met Bouncey.

'As I remember, somebody 'borrowed' some of my magic potion without my permission.'

Bouncey's face turned a bright red.

'I'm sorry. I am really sorry,' he mumbled.

'Don't worry about it, Bouncey. I forgive you,' the Wizard said with a smile.

'Now Trixie, I think you and your friend will need to borrow, with my permission this time, my magic carpet for a while.'

'Wow!' said Bouncey, grinning from ear to ear.

'A magic carpet just for us!'

'Now listen carefully you two,' the Wizard said in a stern voice. 'The magic carpet can only be used by you for twenty four hours before it will return to me all by itself.'

'Flips!' said Bouncey.

'That doesn't give us much time.'

'Only I can control the magic carpet for longer,' the Wizard explained.

'We'll just have to manage,' said Trixie sensibly.

'Now for that potion you wanted, Bouncey.'

As the Wizard went to a shelf at the back of the cave he waved a hand at a large black cat, which was sitting on the shelf.

'Shoo! Shoo!'

The cat slowly turned and looked at the Wizard with two very large green eyes. It stretched out a front paw and began to lick it with a bright pink tongue.

'Shoo! Shoo!' said the Wizard again.

The black cat started to arch its back and hiss through a large open mouth full of sharp teeth.

'Now, now, Ebbo! Don't make a fuss. These people are friends of mine.'

Two large green eyes turned and looked at Trixie and the black cat began to purr, then suddenly jumped to the floor of the cave and walked towards her.

'My word,' said the Wizard. 'Ebbo never usually takes to strangers.'

Of course Trixie had used her special Pixie power to make friends with Ebbo.

Picking up a small dark green bottle, the Wizard turned to Bouncey and smiled.

'I think you still know how to use this, don't you Bouncey?'

'Yes', said Bouncey clicking the fingers of his right hand.
That was the signal to become visible.

The magic potion in the dark green bottle could actually make you invisible.

After thanking the wizard for the magic potion, Bouncey put the small green bottle into his backpack.

He and Trixie then walked towards a brightly coloured carpet, more like a big rug really, placed in the centre of the cave floor, next to the still bubbling cauldron and sat down.

'Now Bouncey,' said the Wizard. 'All you have to do is concentrate and think of where you want to go and the magic carpet will take you there. Oh! And don't forget you can only use the magic carpet for twenty- four hours. It will then come back to me, all right?'

Nodding his head, Bouncey thought hard and ordered the magic carpet to take them towards Mirror Lake.

Slowly and gently the magic carpet rose into the air and flew out of the Wizard's cave.

As they both waved goodbye to the Wizard, Bouncey told Trixie where they were going.

'Why go there first?' asked Trixie.

'I know what's happened,' Bouncey said. The Trolls must have built a wall called a dam across the river. It is stopping all of the water in the river from going down to meet the River of Dreams. They are making another lake as well.'

'Oh! Bouncey. What can we do?' cried Trixie.

'The first thing is to get us down to the ground,' Bouncey said smiling, they had reached the lake as though by magic. He ordered the magic carpet down to a clear space by the river, just next to a dam made of tree logs, which the Trolls had built, just as Bouncey had said. They had packed mud between the logs to stop most of the water getting through.

Bouncey and Trixie looked at what had been done with dismay. On one side of the dam the river was forming into a bigger lake with every minute.

On this side only a small trickle of water could be seen. All of the riverbed could be seen, with just a few small pools filled with fish splashing about inside them.

Trixie looked at Bouncey. 'First we have to help my fish friends before all the water dries up,' she said urgently.

She thought for a minute or two, then said, 'I know who could help us.'

'Great! Who are you thinking about?' asked Bouncey hopefully.

'Just wait a minute please, I'm trying to talk to him,' Trixie replied.

A short time later Bouncey heard a noise coming from the other side of the dam where the river was blocked.

137

A dark, furry whiskered face suddenly appeared on top of the dam.

'It's one of my friends, Nibbles the Beaver,' said Trixie.

'I used my special Pixie powers to ask if he could help us.'

Trixie told Nibbles the Beaver about their problem of how to save the fish in the drying riverbed.

A few moments later a smiling Trixie said to Bouncey, 'Nibbles has agreed to ask his family to help us. He says they can chew the tree trunks and make holes in the dam of logs so the river water will start to flow again and the fish will be saved.'

'Great,' said Bouncey.

'When can they start?'

'Soon,' said Trixie. 'But there is a little problem, it might take more than a day for Nibbles and his family to chew the holes.'

'Well, the sooner you start the sooner you will finish, won't you Nibbles,' Bouncey said as he gave Nibbles a friendly pat on his back.

Nibbles nodded his head in agreement.

Leaving Nibbles to go and get his family, Bouncey and Trixie went back to the magic carpet.

Bouncey concentrated on the directions and the magic carpet flew them up into the air. It carried them both towards the Barren Mountains and the River of Dreams to its beginning. (It's source).

When it began to get dark Bouncey ordered the magic carpet to land by the river for a rest and for something to eat and drink.

'Look how low the river is, Bouncey.' Trixie said. 'The Trolls must have nearly finished the other dam.'

'I'm afraid you might be right,' replied Bouncey. 'Anyway, lets have some food.'

Bouncey opened his backpack and took out a small container. 'I hope you like peanut butter sandwiches, Trixie.'

'Oh yes, I love them. Thonnnk youuu, Bouncey,' said Trixie as she took a big bite of one.

Some time later, Bouncey decided that they would have to stay the night where they were. It was too dark to go on.

Lighting a fire cheered Trixie up. 'I love camp fires,' she told Bouncey. 'They seem so friendly and they do keep you nice and warm.'

Dozing by the fire, Bouncey heard a snuffling noise in the trees behind them.

'Don't move,' he whispered to Trixie. It might be a wild boar.'

'That's all right,' said Trixie, 'my Pixie powers will protect us.'

'Oh! I forgot about them,' Bouncey said. Then he added, 'Just watch this.'

Feeling in his backpack, he pulled out the small green bottle the Wizard had given him earlier.

Opening the top of the bottle, Bouncey took a small sip - and disappeared. He was invisible.

'Where are you?' whispered Trixie.

'Right next to you,' replied Bouncey.

Behind Trixie a big bush twitched and moved and then to her amazement a large wild boar came into view.

One of its ears seemed to be pointing at her and waggling in a strange way. The wild boar sort of walked around the campfire, pulling its head this way and that way but still going round in a circle.

Trixie heard Bouncey laugh even though she could not see him.

'Bouncey! Stop this, at once. It's not funny. Let the wild boar go. Now.' Trixie was furious.

'How could you do such a thing?'

The wild boar gave a loud squeal then rushed off into the woods as Bouncey let it go.

A finger clicked twice and Bouncey reappeared.

'I'm sorry Trixie,' he said. 'That was a bit stupid. I won't do it again.'

'I should hope not,' said Trixie. 'Lets forget it and try to get some sleep.'

The next morning they set off early after Bouncey had ordered the magic carpet to follow the river into the Barren Mountains.

They could see that the river had very little water in it now and they saw more and more little pools full of fish.

'The poor fish won't last long in those small pools, will they Bouncey,' said Trixie in a sad little voice.'

'Don't worry, we'll stop the Trolls,' answered Bouncey with feeling.

'Just you wait and see.'

The magic carpet flew over the nearly dry River of Dreams towards a big mountain. As they got closer they saw that the river came out of a big hole in the side of the mountain.

We shall have to land by that cave thing,' Bouncey said to Trixie.

They had just got off the magic carpet when it suddenly flew back into the air.

'Oh flips!' said Bouncey. 'The twenty-four hours are gone. The Wizard did tell us that the magic carpet would go back by itself, didn't he.'

'Yes he did,' said Trixie. 'What shall we do now?'

They both looked into the darkness of the cave from which only a trickle of water flowed.

'It looks as the though the Trolls have finished making their dam of logs,' said Trixie. 'We're too late.'

'Not if we can knock it down today,' said Bouncey in a fierce voice.

'Come on Trixie, we have to try. Let's see if we can find where the Trolls built their log dam across the river.'

So they slowly walked on the drying riverbed, through a long narrow, dark tunnel.

Suddenly they saw a bright light in the distance. 'That must be the way out,' cried Trixie. 'I'm so glad. I hate this gloomy tunnel.'

What a surprise they got when they got outside. A beautiful valley of trees and glades, each one full of flowers and the sound of birds that could be heard chirping loudly.

'My goodness,' said Bouncey.

'I thought the Barren Mountains had no trees or flowers.'

'This must be a secret valley that no one has ever seen before,' said Trixie excitedly.

Then they saw the river. The River of Dreams was now nearly dry.

'We shall have to go pretty quickly if we are to do something,' said Bouncey urgently..

141

Just then they heard a cry for help. Not far in front of them was a big rock. Lying down in front of it was the strangest creature Bouncey and Trixie had ever seen.

It had arms and legs, which seemed to be tied up. On the back of its body were two strange looking wings, attached to a box-like thing. Lines of string were tied to the arms and legs and most strange of all the face was covered with a shiny glass mask.

'I say can you help me?' A voice said from behind the mask.

'My name is Glyde and I have hurt my foot.'

'Wow,' said Bouncey.

'It's a person.'

'I'm not a person, I'm a Flip-Flap.'

Trixie rushed over to Glyde and asked him to let her look at his injured foot.

All pixies have a special power to make any person or animal better if they have been hurt.

Trixie also carried in her waist pouch, a special ointment, which can cure most cuts and bruises very quickly.

After taking off Glyde's shoe and sock, Trixie rubbed some of her special ointment on his injured ankle.

'Hey!' he said.

'It feels better already.'

He looked at them closely and said, 'Where are you from then? You don't look like Flip-Flaps.'

'No we're not,' said Bouncey and he told Glyde all about the Trolls and the river.

'Oh! We know all about the Trolls,' Glyde said.

'Drygon the giant Ogre sent them. They're his slaves you know.'

'No, we didn't know,' said Bouncey and Trixie together.

'Well, when the Trolls started to build a log dam across the river we, the Flip-Flaps didn't know what to do. The Trolls are very fierce and we are afraid of them.'

'Fierce or not,' Bouncey said. 'We have come to stop them and pull down their dam of logs across the river.

'Now then Glyde, do you think the Flip-Flaps will help us? I mean you don't really know us, do you?'

'Yes we will. I'm sure we will. All of the Flip-Flaps want to get rid of the horrible Trolls.'

Now feeling much better, Glyde put his sock and shoe back on and then he stood up with his wings sticking out behind him.

Glyde then showed Bouncey and Trixie how his wings worked.

By pulling the line fixed to his wrists the wings moved up. Then bending his legs like a frog jumping, the wings moved down.

'Of course you have to do it fairly quickly after you have jumped up, to start flying into the air,' he said.

Then Glyde shouted, 'Follow me. I will fly very slowly.'

Bouncey and Trixie watched as Glyde jumped into the air and pulled his arms out and after bending his knees, kick his legs straight.

Flip-Flap, Flip-Flap, his wings clapped each time they moved up and down.

'So that's why they are called Flip-Flaps,' laughed Trixie.

Flying above them Glyde led Bouncey and Trixie along a path by the now dried up river.

Soon the sides of the river grew taller and taller until the sky seemed to be miles above them.

Then the side of the river they were walking along suddenly became like a giant cliff. It was so steep it seemed impossible for anyone to climb it.

'Nearly there,' cried Glyde, Flip-Flapping above them.

Bouncey looked up and was amazed to see windows and doorways all over the cliff.

'You, you don't live up there do you?' asked Trixie, her eyes wide open in astonishment.

'Of course we do,' replied Glyde. 'It's nice and safe from the horrible Trolls.'

'Well,' said Bouncey. 'It's all right for you. What about us? How do we get up there?'

'No problem at all,' said Glyde. 'We had to make steps for the young ones and for the old who cannot fly.'

'Flips,' said Bouncey.

'I don't like the thought of climbing up those steps.'

'And me,' Trixie muttered to herself. 'I don't think I could fly so near to that cliff wall without getting dizzy.'

Glyde said that they had only five floors to climb and they would be all right.

After a horrible ten minutes of creeping slowly up the steep stone steps they reached the fifth floor and went inside Glyde's house.

It was just like any other house except that from the window there was nothing but the river, straight down, five floors below them.

Glyde had got there first, having flown in through his front door and had set out some food and drink for them.

144

'I'm starving,' said Bouncey as he bit into a large sarnie of something strange but which was very tasty.

'Me too,' Trixie said as she munched a big orange and green cake. 'Ummmm - this is delicious.'

'We've no time to waste,' Bouncey said after a big swallow of a blue coloured fizzy drink.

'We have to pull the Troll's log dam down as soon as is possible and let the River of Dreams flow again.'

Glyde said he would get some of his friends and then they would make a plan.

Soon afterwards Glyde and his friends told Bouncey and Trixie of an idea they had thought of.

First Glyde showed Bouncey and Trixie his strange face-mask. 'This is made from the Bubble Tree seed case,' he explained.

'Once a year, the Bubble tree makes hundreds of tiny bubble seed cases. When they grow to the size of your head, the bubble splits and the seed is thrown to the ground. Now, the thing is this. The bubble seed case is very sticky.'

'Actually,' said Glyde.

'Your hands would be stuck together for weeks if you didn't take care when touching them. We use a special chalk powder to dust our hands, before we touch a bubble seed case.'

'Confidentially,' Glyde added. 'A stretched and dried bubble seed case is like a kind of glass but much stronger. Our wings are made from it as well. And the Bubble tree is growing it's seed cases now.'

'That's just what we want,' said Bouncey. 'Something to stop the Trolls but without hurting them.'

'What about the log dam?' asked Trixie. 'How are we going to pull it down?'

'I've been thinking about that,' said Bouncey.

'We only need to pull down a small part of it, otherwise we could cause a big flood if all of the log dam was pulled down at the same time.'

'That's right,' said Glyde. 'It's a good job you thought of that. We might have caused a lot more damage to the people living downriver.'

145

About half an hour later, Glyde and his friends were showing Bouncey and Trixie the place where the Trolls had built the log dam.

'It's big isn't it?' whispered Trixie.

The log dam stretched across the river, from one bank to the other. Behind it the river was flooding the farmland for as far as they could see.

On their side, only a few small pools of water could be seen. Fish were desperately splashing about in them.

Not far from where they were watching a gang of Trolls were rolling more tree logs towards the river.

'They must be going to make the log dam even higher,' said Glyde in a worried voice. 'We've got to do it now.'

'Okay,' said Bouncey. 'Give me two minutes and then get ready to fly.'

'Right,' said Glyde and his friends nodded in agreement.

Bouncey slid down the small hill that they had been hiding on and stopped to get his green bottle of magic potion out of his backpack.

Opening the green bottle Bouncey took a little sip - and disappeared. Without being seen, of course, he walked towards the Trolls. When he was quite close to them he clicked his fingers twice and reappeared.

The Trolls were at first startled to see Bouncey appear from nowhere. Then with a great roar they all rushed to catch him.

Bouncey was ready for them. He took another sip from the green bottle and disappeared again.

The Trolls were furious. They all rushed towards the nearest trees, thinking Bouncey had hidden himself amongst them.

Actually Bouncey had run to the log dam and feeling into his backpack, pulled out a small hammer and a handful of hooks.

Very carefully he crawled along the log dam then stopped and began to knock an eye-hook into six of the logs. Then he crawled back to the riverbank.

Clicking his fingers twice Bouncey reappeared again. Loud cries and shouts made him look towards the trees.

Flip-Flapping above them were Glyde and his friends. They were throwing sticky Bubble Tree seed cases onto the Trolls.

They began shouting and howling but couldn't get free from the sticky Bubble Tree seed cases. Hands, feet and even two Trolls were stuck together.

'Leave them for now,' shouted Bouncey. 'Lets fix the log dam.'

So Glyde and his friends Flip-Flapped over to where Bouncey had knocked the hooks into the logs.

Each one had another hook tied to a thin rope. Taking turns, Glyde and his friends lowered their hooks and because they were also magnets, they hooked up quite easily.

Then, all together, Glyde and his friends began to Flip-Flap faster and faster, pulling the logs to which they were hooked.

Trixie was jumping and flying little hops at the same time, as she clapped her hands and shouted, 'PULL! Glyde! PULL!'

Bouncey watched with his fingers crossed for luck. Then with a loud squelchey sluuurp, the logs began to move. Water squirted out like a fountain from the gaps, which could now be seen in the dam.

Suddenly, all six logs popped out of the dam and the river water rushed through the gap and started to fill the riverbed but without causing a flood.

'We've done it! We've done it,' shouted Trixie, as Bouncey gave Glyde and his friends a grin and waved his hands in a big thank you.

Glyde waved back as he and his friends cut the ropes hooked to the logs and then watched as the logs floated away down the river.

The River of Dreams had been saved.

Later on, Glyde and his friends cleaned up the Trolls from the sticky Bubble seed cases using their special chalk powder.

The Trolls were afraid of going back to Drygon, the giant Ogre because of what had happened to the log dams.

So The Flip-Flaps decided to let them stay as long as the Trolls helped to repair any flood damage they had caused.

The Trolls were so glad that they were no longer slaves of Drygon the Ogre they agreed that they would stay to help.

Bouncey and Trixie said goodbye to Glyde and his friends. They were sorry that they had to leave the Flip-Flaps but hoped to return one day.

Glyde was pleased to have met some new friends and that the Flip-Flaps had made friends with the Trolls as well.

After waving good-bye, on a log raft made by some of the Trolls, Bouncey and Trixie sat comfortably in the chairs made from Bubble seed case material and floated slowly homewards down the River of Dreams.

They were very pleased to see Nibbles the Beaver with his family as they floated past the smaller river flowing down from Mirror Lake.

Nibbles and his family had managed to chew through the log dam and make the river flow again just in time.

Floating down the River of Dreams, now not far from home and the Sleep Tree, Bouncey thought how lucky he was to have such good friends.

Especially the ones who had helped him save the River of Dreams.

The Author

Watercolour painting by Rita Clements Lee

ritaclementslee-artist.co.uk/